Don't Drink and Fly

The Story of Bernice O'Hanlon
Part One

Don't Drink and Fly

The Story of Bernice O'Hanlon
Part One

Cathie Devitt

Winchester, UK
Washington, USA

First published by Roundfire Books, 2014
Roundfire Books is an imprint of John Hunt Publishing Ltd., Laurel House, Station Approach,
Alresford, Hants, SO24 9JH, UK
office1@jhpbooks.net
www.johnhuntpublishing.com
www.roundfire-books.com

For distributor details and how to order please visit the 'Ordering' section on our website.

Text copyright: Cathie Devitt 2014
www.cathiedevitt.com

ISBN: 978 1 78279 016 7

A CIP catalogue record for this book is available from the British Library.

Design: Stuart Davies

Printed in the USA by Edwards Brothers Malloy

CONTENTS

This book is dedicated to:
My dad, who listened to me, and is always with me. My mum, who is my role model and always encouraged me. My daughters Cassandra and Megan-Rose, who always believed in me.

Preface

My aim was to write the story of Bernice in a way that would be accessible and show the highs and lows of everyday life as a witch living in Glasgow; away from home, holding down a job, dealing with relationships and harbouring a sense of loss and frustration from her past.

Bernice is a complex character. Don't judge her actions too harshly.

This novel has been gathering dust under my bed. When I started writing it I was bursting with ideas and enthusiasm. I fear that I listened too much to the opinion of others and spent more time reading "how to craft a novel" books and less time actually crafting this novel. I know how to write to a formula, I just don't want to.

I finally decided that I would imitate Frank Sinatra and "do it my way". This being a tribute to my wonderful dad and his amazing brother, my Uncle Vinny as this iconic song was a favourite of theirs and the lyrics are so apt.

I left school at 16, bored and frustrated at the lack of enthusiasm from teachers to encourage creativity and recognise achievable aspirations. I did eventually succumb to the pressures of working life and successfully completed various further education courses including a University Degree, Diploma and several HNCs. As interesting as the courses were, they have not lit up my life the way that creative writing does.

This is the first in a series about Bernice.

Foreword

Cathie Devitt lives and breathes stories. Every conversation leads to another story, then another and another, each as original, entertaining and thought-provoking as the last. Her writing is similarly engaging, with characters as memorable as their author in settings and situations unique to Cathie's world view. Her short stories are bursting with energy and life. At last we have that long-awaited debut novel.

Lindsay Fraser: Literary Agent.

Acknowledgments

Thank You...

Pauline Reid www.bewitchingbeauty.co.uk for letting me into your Pagan world, circle of friends and fantastic home which is a shrine to the craft, and of course for the hydro facials and hot stone massages.

Mandy Sinclair www.mandysinclair.com for the fabulous cover illustration and your delectable company over cakes and Cava.

Lindsey Fraser www.fraserross.co.uk for trying to mould me into literary acceptability over many lunches in Edinburgh and Glasgow. (Told you I was a rebel.)

Lucy Greeves www.lucygreeves.com for introducing me to Hatha Yoga. I never fell asleep once in the meditation sessions.

Scottish Book Trust www.scottishbooktrust.com for allowing me to take in part in the New Writer Mentoring programme.

Arvon Foundation www.arvon.org/centres/totleigh-barton/ for the bursary that allowed me time and space to complete the final edit on this novel.

John Hunt Publishing www.johnhuntpublishing.com for the time and patience of your editorial and production staff.

Introduction

West Coast of Scotland

Bernice stretched sleepily in a cave, woken by the hungry scream of seagulls drowning the whispering of an early tide.

It was a beautiful morning, despite damp sand clinging to her clothes. She pushed a tangle of paprika curls behind one ear, lightly touched the amulet around her neck and smiled. She always wore the silver pentacle.

Gathering her bits and bobs from the previous night's incantation, Bernice looped her sandals through manicured fingertips and ambled along the shoreline. Sea foam trickled like cold cappuccino over her bare toes.

She paused for a moment to admire the sunrise. Fuschian violet dripped from an amber smudge, spilling onto inky water. The sea rippled as light danced like will o' the wisps over its surface.

Bernice inhaled the salty air and looked towards the streets. Windows glowed in a few guest houses, where stalwarts of the area prepared to welcome their elderly clientele. Faded saltire bunting drooped around a small ice-cream kiosk luring tourists to enjoy the area.

Bernice headed for the promenade, leaving footprints in the sand as she headed back to the grime of the city.

Chapter 1

The landlord described Bernice's flat as small but quirky. The rent was fair for Glasgow city centre and the ideal location for her above the salon where she worked. The quirkiness Bernice loved. The dinkiness meant a carpet of Bernice's shoes adorned the communal hallway giving rise to gossip of her attempt to put the local mosque out of business.

No two windows were the same shape. An Aga set into the wall replaced a baker's oven previously used to serve the community. Three half-moon stairs led to Bernice's living area. It was here she rested on an overstuffed sofa, confident of the success of the previous night's ritual at the beach.

Bernice wound a few strands of coppery curls around her fingers, and fell into a deep sleep.

She usually dreamt in colour, but this morning the palette bore shades of grey. She dreamt of the mother she knew only from photographs, a lone soul at the edge of the sea. Bernice wondered at the strength of the waves, the melody of surf brushing against the rocks. The contrast of water being both healing and fatal intrigued her.

She was comfortable on the sofa as her subconscious combed her imagination.

As she dreamt, Bernice was drawn to murky waters where her mother stood cradling an infant wrapped in a pale shawl. As Bernice approached with outstretched arms, the image faded. The waves grew higher, darker and more menacing as a cruel wind whipped the waters to frenzy. Bernice heard a muffled cry and felt herself falling.

She woke with a start, sticky with sweat and lying on her living-room floor. Hex jumped to safety the way cats do. Bernice sat upright. She shivered, content her son was safe.

It was time for Bernice to face her past. Bernice held a small angelite crystal in the palm of her hand. She closed her fingers over it for a few seconds and let her mind drift back to when she was eight years old.

It was a warm summer's day. Waving to Granny, Bernice skipped down the worn path outside the smallholding where they lived. She glanced around quickly making sure no one saw her and slipped quietly into the belly of the woods tracing a familiar path, past the burnt-out hollow of the big oak, across a carpet of bluebells, carefully stepping over the shallow stream towards her den. Four huge boulders lay embedded in the soil. Their humpbacked curves offering hours of adventure to the imaginative eight-year-old. This was her secret place.

Bernice felt safe. The silence broken only by the occasional rustle of leaves or twigs snapping underfoot as she busied herself creating the day's adventure. The secret place was ideal for her dolly's hospital. Bernice dropped her rucksack heavily to the ground.

A scrunched-up bag of "odd fellows" spilled over onto the damp grass. The pastel lozenges scattered like a rainbow jigsaw. She popped a bright pink sweetie into her mouth, luxuriating in pleasure as the clove flavouring trickled down the back of her throat.

Plunging deeper into the bag she rescued Uncle Ted, Miffy, and Lino the lion, along with a selection of small blankets and the dented biscuit tin with her first-aid kit packed inside. She treated Ted to a crepe bandage turban whilst Miffy got off with a sticking plaster on each knee. Bernice tucked a small plastic thermometer under Lino's front paw and dabbed a cotton pad, moistened with spittle, at his fevered brow. So lost in her role as nurse the little girl didn't realise how late it was.

The sky grew darker to a mushy grey, like God forgot to put a coin in the meter. Bernice packed up her things and headed home. She didn't notice the stump of a tree trunk and toppled down a steep embankment. It all happened so quickly, she didn't have time to be scared. But she was afraid now.

"Jack and Jill went up the hill..." she whispered, focused on the expanse of water stretching out beyond her. Bernice was a regular

visitor to the seaside but she never knew the sea reached all the way up here. Further along a cluster of woodland meant shelter.

She stumbled across the sands towards the protection of the trees. Bernice trundled on, keeping to the edge of the beach, the contrast of sand and soil merging, reminding her of the wonders of Mother Nature. The air was damp. It was getting darker now. Instinctively she pulled her cardigan tighter across her chest. Droplets of rain mingled with tears as branches scratched and clawed at her face. She frantically pushed them aside in her quest to find the way home. The sun struggled to penetrate the barrier of trees as they fought for space in the density of the woods. She would rest a while before retracing her footsteps back along the shore. Her ankle strained against the strap of her sandals as she tried cautiously to move forward. Twigs snapped underfoot. The trees loomed high above her head. The breeze slowed to a halt, Bernice dared not move. She leaned against a massive old Wyche elm and tried to catch her breath. Her feet were numb. Looking down at her bare toes she thought of snakes and wished she hadn't worn the red plastic sandals.

The soft mohair of her cardigan clung to her like a second skin. Damp from sweat, she felt light-headed and slid down to sit on the grass. The bark of the tree was rough. Slowly she turned towards it.

She vaguely remembered nature talks from school and wondered how old the tree was? How long was it stood here? A silent witness. Witness to what she wondered? An army of ants scurried nearby.

How easy it would be to wipe them out with one hard stamp of those red sandals. How vulnerable they looked. Totally oblivious they continued, meticulously manoeuvring a piece of crab-apple.

Bernice was surprised by her own cruel thoughts. She too felt vulnerable in the past but this was fear, nauseating fear. If she wasn't at the table when Granddad got home she knew she was in for real trouble.

Seeking shelter in the shade of the huge tree, Bernice wrapped herself as best she could in the dolly blankets. She reached for a small boulder and felt its weight in her hand, cool and smooth, her protection from anything bigger than ants. She was tired but knew she couldn't rest for *long.*

The rain was falling in cold sheets over her. She licked tears and rain from trembling lips. Glancing back, she thought she could make out a figure slumped at the edge of the beach. It lay motionless as the water lapped around. Soon the tide would rise, and the body would be washed away. Who knew how long it would take to find? Bernice rubbed at her tired eyes and tried to stay calm, hoping the increasing rain would extinguish her vivid imagination.

"Shadows. Shadows. Trick of the light," she convinced herself.

She must have dozed off, because the next thing she knew Granddad was shaking her arm roughly.

"Bloody pest, how many times have we told you not to go wandering off?"

Granny stood behind him, twisting the gold band on her finger.

"Thank God she's safe wid ye?" The old woman fell to her knees in front of Bernice and began rubbing the child's arms briskly, to get her circulation going. "Cuddle into me, Bernadette."

Bernice snuggled her tiny frame under the big crocheted blanket Granny used since she was a baby. Squares of surplus wool from the many fine garments Granny knitted over the years. The magic blanket believed to cure all ailments. Granny wrapped the blanket around her like a shawl and scooped her granddaughter into her arms. Bernice rested her chin on Granny's shoulder.

Was that a woman standing by the shore?

Granny stopped briefly, realising how close they were to where Bernice's mother was found almost a decade earlier, tangled in the seaweed, dragged her to her death.

Granny shivered, at the memory of losing her daughter, thankful Bernice was in her life. The old woman tightened her grip and clung to her tremulous frame as the child looked over her shoulder, mesmerised by the lights from the retreating sun, flickering off the canvas of the sea.

The woman was gone.

Hex scratched at an envelope on the mat. The note was lying behind Bernice's front door. The writing was childish. Large print on a crumpled envelope. The pencilled words were scrawled in an awkward angle across the back.

"I know where your son is." A post office box number was scratched beneath the cryptic message. First instalment to be sent and more information would follow.

'It says what?' Maggie's voice croaked as she answered Bernice's phone call. She rubbed at sleep and mascara to unglue her eyes.

'Someone must know something.'

'Or someone is playing a sick joke.' Maggie sat up quickly.

'Or maybe their conscience has held the secret for long enough?'

'But who else would know where the baby was buried? You tried the Registrars and got nothing.'

'He must be somewhere. I'd have somewhere to go, to be near him. It all makes sense.'

'Bernice, if your granddad never registered the birth, he is hardly likely to have registered the death, it's a sick hoax. We'll talk later.'

* * *

Taking a notepad and pen, Bernice let the words tumble from her heart to the page. Many moons had passed since Bernice moved to Glasgow but still she wrote. One day Granny would reply. Then Bernice would go back.

Chapter 2

In a cottage in the Scottish Highlands, Dermott Flannigan sat staring at his hands. He held a small bundle of unopened letters. Rain battered the single sash window behind him. Despite the sender's name being clearly written on the back of each envelope, the letters were never addressed to their intended recipient.

He scratched his chin and sighed. 'Ach, Bernadette, Jeez.'

The undertaker explained what paperwork was needed to register the death; make the arrangements. Presuming the next of kin was too overcome with grief, the task was suggested to Dermott to deal with.

Dermott tucked the letters back under the lid of the rusted biscuit tin he'd found them in and shoved it behind an old wooden trunk.

A voice bellowed from below. 'What is yon eejit doing up there! Get the fecking thing and let's get this sorted! Even now the auld besom is keeping me from me business.' An old man was struggling to stand, pushing a wheelchair away from him.

'Please take the chair. You're not fit...' His companion flushed, grabbing the chair. 'At least take this.'

'Out of me way, Robbie,' the old man growled. He leaned heavily on the chair and clung to the stick being offered. 'I'll decide whether I'm fit or not! I make the fecking decisions around here! Put a roof over your heads didn't I! Raised you like my own! Ungrateful pair of gob-shites!'

Dermott watched from the attic window. The old man looked towards the skylight.

'Get a move on, eejit!' The voice from the yard sounded stronger than the body it came from.

The journey was short, conversation sparse. They pulled the car into a driveway. A man's legs poked out from the cab of an elegant hearse, clouds of smoke escaping from within. He quickly stubbed out his cigarette and waved at the air above his knees before producing a chamois leather and rubbing aimlessly at the ink-black paintwork.

'Ah, gentlemen.' The chamois was left on the car's bonnet as the trio were escorted inside.

'Right, let's get it over with,' the old man rasped.

'Ah, thank you for being so prompt, may I offer you tea? Something stronger?'

'I'll have the something stronger. Why I need to be here at all I don't know.' The old man accepted a tumbler of whisky. He drained the glass.

'Ah, refill? Yes, this is a very difficult time for you.'

'Sort him out, Dermott.'

Dermott laid a sheaf of documents on the funeral director's desk. 'I think it's all here, what your man put on the list like.'

'She had a good innings then.'

'Lazy good for nothing, sucked the life out of me I'll tell you. Poor stock her family. I married the runt of the litter and it only got worse from there on in,' the old man slurred.

'Date of death…I need a signature here…and here…'

The old man scrawled his name twice and banged the tumbler down. 'Enough then? All done?'

'She was an angel.' Robbie snuffled into a handkerchief.

'Fecking witch I tell you.'

'I'm sorry.' Dermott apologised as Robbie helped the old man out to the car.

'No problem, grief affects people in many ways. You've sorted the service?'

Dermott nodded. 'And the music, she loved her music.'

The undertaker took Dermott's hand in a firm grip and patted his back. 'You've done well. She'd be so proud. Go easy on your father.'

The car horn sounded.

'He's not my father.' Dermott walked towards the car.

Chapter 3

Bernice's friend Maggie was busy in her kitchen. She shuffled around bags of groceries, stopping only to swallow her third painkiller of the day. Bernice's instructions were clear.

'Get the kettle on, I'll be over in a jiffy.' Then the phone line went dead.

All too soon for Maggie, her friend was there, kicking off her shoes at the back door. She thrust the letter at Maggie.

'Sick joke, Bernice.' Maggie took the letter and tossed it into the open bin, she closed the lid. Bernice moved towards the bin.

'Leave it!' Maggie barked.

'Did you catch the documentary?' Bernice changed the subject quickly.

'Yes.'

'Did you see it though? Total eclipse! I've never seen anything like it.'

Maggie concentrated on loading tins into cupboards. 'It was all right. Went a bit dark. Sort of spooky.'

'Nothing spooky about it.' Bernice leaned against the breakfast bar. 'It was brilliant. You'll never see such a sight again in our lifetime.' She stroked a corn dolly pinned to the wall. 'I think it's a sign.'

'We didn't actually see it, Bernice.'

'Near enough. I saw the moon last night at the beach. Same moon. Got me thinking, about family, then this letter turns up.'

'You are wired to the moon.'

'I wish you would chill out,' Bernice said quietly. 'I gave you the corn dolly for a reason. Lammas was the time to count your blessings, appreciate the positives in life. You never listen.'

Maggie sighed and pushed past armed with several boxes of cereal.

'Lammas Pammas. Christmas and Easter is more than

9

enough, Bernice. Some of us don't have time for any more celebrations.'

'I thought you liked it?' Bernice flicked the dolly's feet.

'It's lovely, Bernice. It's a straw doll. Not a God.' Maggie scowled.

'It's more than a doll. It symbolises a new harvest, gratitude...'

'You are always talking about the moon and the stars, Bernice. It's time you came down to earth and got your act together, never mind having your head in the clouds all the time.'

Bernice chewed the end of her hair.

Maggie sighed. 'Okay, Bernice. I'm sorry. Forget about the letter, honestly, forget it. I don't have time to talk about it.'

'You put the rest of the groceries away.' Bernice dropped two tea bags into chunky mugs and switched on the kettle.

Maggie busied herself with the rest of the shopping.

'Where was your brain when you went out?' Bernice held up a large bag of tangerines and laughed.

'Yes, okay. My mind's on other things.'

'On other things?' Bernice suggested, more gently. She hooked a finger into the red netting and let the fruit fall onto the worktop. 'Must have been.'

Maggie said nothing as she drowned the tea bags with hot water.

Bernice was counting under her breath. 'Twenty-four wee oranges,' she crowed. 'Enough to prevent scurvy in a shipload of sailors.'

'Yes, all right! Give me a break will you? I'm running around like the proverbial blue-arsed fly while you stand there, making wisecracks!'

There was a groan from the direction of the hallway.

'Should you two not be working?' Maggie's husband, just woken from a brief sleep at the end of his night shift stood in underpants scratching his crotch.

'I did tell you I've taken the day off, Wredd, last night?'

'Jeez!' Bernice covered her nose and mouth with her hand. 'I smell death. How is life at the abattoir then?'

'Hilarious. I've told you it's a food processing plant,' Wredd growled. 'I want a drink and then I'm going for a shower.'

Maggie turned to Bernice. 'Why are you not at the salon?'

Bernice shrugged. 'Sorry, babes. I can't be bothered with all the stocktaking malarkey. I'll do it tomorrow.'

Wredd shook his head slowly. Maggie folded her arms tightly across her midriff.

'Great. Terrific. McIntosh will go berserk.'

'It's fine. I'll shuffle a few things around, get the junior to count stuff. It'll be fine.'

Wredd opened the fridge door and gulped from a carton.

'Need to slush the blood and guts off me then I'm away back to bed.'

'Spark me up, Maggie?' Bernice held a king-size filter cigarette between red-tipped fingers.

'I gave it up remember? Thought you'd done the same, Bernice.'

'Been feeling a bit stressed.' Bernice paused. 'My boy would be eighteen this year.' She sighed. 'Do you think the letter is for real?'

Maggie sighed too. 'Look, I know it must be hard, you're still young enough to meet a nice guy, maybe have more kids. The letter was a sick joke.'

'Maybe you're right but the old clock is ticking. There are no "nice" guys, believe me. I'll end up known as the wacky witch who talks to her cat.'

'Lots of folk talk to their pets. I even talk to Hex, it's not just you.'

'Sure, but now he's answering back.' Bernice laughed. 'Any matches then? This thing's empty.' She slid a lighter into her pocket. Maggie looked on as Bernice opened the back door and leant against it, looking towards the garden.

Maggie threw a box of matches towards her. Bernice took a slow defiant drag on her cigarette. 'Been thinking about home a lot recently.' Bernice stretched to reach her mug of tea. 'You know, thinking, about stuff. Maybe it's time to go home, face the old man. Find out the truth.'

Maggie sighed and pressed her fingers against her forehead. 'Can we talk later, Bernice? I've got my own problems right now.'

'What? The Prince of Darkness through there? Kick him to the kerb.'

Maggie clasped a hand across her mouth and rushed out of the room. After a few minutes Bernice stubbed out her cigarette, retrieved the letter from the bin, and followed her.

'You feel sick again?' she called through the bathroom door. A moment passed and Bernice knocked on the door. 'I'll away then, Maggie, let you catch a sleep.'

'Wait,' Maggie croaked. 'Hold on a minute.' The snib rattled. 'Forget about the letter. Leave the past where it is.'

'The thing though. Until I know where he rests, I can't. I felt different last night, at the beach.'

'Last night?' Maggie rubbed her forehead. 'Oh, Bernice, you'll get arrested one of these days, all this nonsense faffing about in caves in your bare scud. I wouldn't have thought you'd have anything but contempt for the sea, after what happened to your mother.'

'Listen, Tabitha.' Bernice twitched her nostrils. 'Have faith in your Aunt Endora. There's magic in those waters.'

'Tabitha was the daughter in the TV show, Samantha the mother.' Maggie sighed. 'Some witch you are.'

'Whatever. I don't always know which witch is which but I do know what's what. You're as pale as Morticia. You get your head down.' Bernice rubbed Maggie's arm. 'Get the useless big lump to help more.'

Bernice hesitated before pulling a woollen scarf from a hook on the front door and stuffing it into her handbag.

'Get him told.' Bernice cocked her head towards the stairs. 'Come to mine tomorrow.'

At last Maggie felt the peace and quiet she craved. She plodded across the hallway to the spare bedroom, her earlier conversation with Wredd still on her mind.

* * *

'I married you, Maggie, not you're screwed-up friend. Send her back to the Highlands or planet Zanussi. Get her out of our lives would you?'

Maggie pleaded, 'Try and understand. She's going through a bad patch.'

'No, Maggie! We're going through a bad patch, and she is the cause of it. You know, when we first met I thought it was great the way you two were so close, now I'm beginning to wonder if there's more to it?'

'Don't start again. Bernice is as much lesbian as you are Alsatian.'

'Oh really? So how come she can't hold onto a man? How come she's never married? Nick did ask her, though I'm still not sure he plays for the blue team.'

'You are such a narrow-minded chauvinistic pig! She has a lot of issues,' Maggie sobbed, hating the confrontation. 'Nick is more man than you'll ever be.'

'Right, here we go, turn on the waterworks. Poor Bernice. Give us both a break. She's a time-bomb. Can't you see what she's doing?'

* * *

Maggie reached for a tub of tiger balm and scooped a little from it. She inhaled the sharp smell of eucalyptus and rubbed her temples firmly.

A small photograph on a bedside table showed the threesome in happier times; laughing into the camera. Maggie glanced briefly at the table. A gold-mesh pouch held a selection of trinkets; candles, crystals, incense and a parchment scroll – a spell written for Maggie. Next to it, a half-melted candle settled beside a hump of incense ash, on top of a pile of paperwork. Maggie sighed at her own little mountain of unpaid debt. Bernice's gift only added to her housework.

Maggie pulled down the blackout blind, rested for a few seconds to adjust her eyes to the change of light and felt her way to the empty bed. Curling her knees towards her chin, she pulled a pillow to hug.

With one ear cocked for Wredd wakening and his imminent demand for dinner Maggie ran a finger across the photo-frame.

'Total eclipse rights enough, Bernice.' She sighed, and tucked her nose beneath the duvet breathing in the freshness of the linen.

Chapter 4

Bernice glanced back at Maggie's house as blinds in the ground-floor bedroom closed. She noticed a figure at the window above. Wredd stared down at her, a towelling robe draped around his shoulders. She strained to make eye contact. He dropped the robe. She turned her back on him and walked towards the bus stop still in his line of vision. Her best friend's husband? Bernice shivered.

She pulled Wredd's football scarf from her bag and looped it around her neck, turned back, blew him a kiss and waved.

Several taxis sat on the rank. The driver grunted as Bernice slid into the front seat beside him.

'Shopping centre please,' she asked, pulling down the vanity mirror to check her lip gloss.

'Been waiting for a call since seven this morning, and now you only want to go to the precinct?'

'What?' She turned to look straight at him, taking in the walnut face with its deep furrowed brow.

'I'm only saying. You could walk. I've not been on an airport run all week.'

'Wait a minute then...' She stalled for time, and gathered a few select items from around her, as he squeaked a finger across the windscreen at some invisible smear.

Bernice slowly opened the car door. 'Think I'll walk after all.'

'Time wasters... I aye mind a face.' Shaking his head, he leant across and pulled the door closed. Bernice stood by the side of the road and patted her bulging satchel.

'Bloody men,' she muttered, 'think they rule the world.' Anger building with each step, she walked towards a small bank of shops.

'Never heard the likes. Driver went off like a firework,' she told the manager of the wine merchants. He was chewing a pen, his eyes fixed on a small TV screen. Bernice set two bottles on the counter.

Still occupied by the sports channel, he swiped her credit card and pulled a plastic bag from the holder.

'I know. Double bag, in case it rips,' he said without looking at her.

'Because they are so flimsy.'

'Bottles are heavy.'

'Okay, Einstein.'

He re-focused on the afternoon's horse racing. An open newspaper lay across the counter. The chewed pen lay on top. Several names were circled. Bernice scribbled across the page and slipped his pen into her carrier bag.

'Bye then!' she called to the back of the wine merchant's head.

A man leaned against a bus stop, watching Bernice. Half hidden by an umbrella, his eyes followed her as she walked away from the shop, he trailed behind.

Chapter 5

Hex stirred when he heard Bernice's key in the lock.

'Where's my babee?' Bernice cooed. The cat curled his back and stretched. Bernice tossed her jacket onto a small console. 'What a day, Hex. See people. See men?' She relayed the earlier events to a cat interested only in having his dishes replenished. Hex watched as she restocked a small metal wine rack. Bernice slopped food and water into the cat's dishes. She pulled open a drawer. Amongst spare plugs and scraps of string Bernice found what she was looking for. The corkscrew made her smile every time she used it.

'It's like a tiny tin man holding his arms up and surrendering,' she once said to Maggie. 'If only all men were so obliging.' She poured a large glass of red wine and headed for the sofa.

Bob Dylan kept Bernice company all afternoon. His gravelly tone massaged her ears as she cradled the sweet drink, sipping in time with the dirge of the album. Hex settled contentedly at her feet, disturbed only when she reached for the bookcase behind the sofa. Bernice chose two books from her collection.

The book on Wicca was a gift from her granny along with a delightful angelite crystal, both hidden at the bottom of a small suitcase packed for Bernice's move to Glasgow. Bernice used the guide still.

Years before, Bernice followed the author's advice of creating her own book of shadows: a journal of her practiced spells detailing her thoughts and feelings and the results that followed.

Bernice's book of shadows was a thick sheaf of recycled paper bound in a slate cover fastened by thick leather ribbon. The front cover was studded with semi-precious gems embossed around the edges. Inside the centre pages, flowing from a scribbled mind map, was pasted several photos of a boy with hot paprika curls. Cut from magazines, the images followed a time-line from birth onwards.

'It's your birthday soon.' Bernice pressed the wine glass to her lips. 'Let me know where you are?'

Close inspection would show the pictures were not of the same child, but in Bernice's eyes this was a visual diary of her son's life as she imagined it would have been.

At the centre of the map written in her finest calligraphy were the words "Always have hope" coiled around a tiny red love-heart. Bernice rested, flicking through the pages, stopping occasionally to wipe a tear or catch her breath in laughter. The book was a diary of Bernice's spiritual life.

After some time poring over her memoirs, Bernice closed the book and mulled over how different her life might have been if her son lived, if her mother lived, if her granddad died and left them all in peace. Bernice imagined her aura turn angry red.

'Purple, blue, lilac, colour me white.' Bernice pressed her palms together and taking a deep breath, repeated the mantra over and over until she felt her spirit restored.

The day passed with a calmness Bernice had not experienced in a while. The windows of her small flat welcomed evening shadows as she moved towards an old beanbag in the corner of the room. She settled cross-legged on the worn fabric. Pushing up the sleeves of her loose top she remembered a recent experience with a toppled cauldron. It caused no end of confusion for her distressed insurance company. The last thing she wanted was to explain more burnt clothing. She carefully lit a cluster of thick candles and considered an appropriate spell to cast.

Soothed by the music still playing on a loop, Bernice closed her eyes, her hands rested upturned on her knees, feet tucked beneath the velvet layers of her skirt. She inhaled the sweet scent of patchouli and recalled her negative encounters earlier in the day; Wredd, the taxi driver, the shopkeeper. She justified a process of elimination that made sense to her.

'Airport run?' She sighed, arranging various small objects

along an altar of purple velvet; a business card, the discarded ring from the cabby's coke can, and a few hairs from the jacket hanging on the back of his seat. *I'll send you flying alright,* she thought.

With a shawl of calm caressing her body Bernice performed her chosen ritual. Satisfied, she snuffed what remained of the candles and scooped the trinkets into a box studded with bruised shades of onyx.

Placing the box in Hex's litter tray, she wrapped her offerings neatly with his, inside the newspaper lining, and headed out to the backyard.

Clawing the soft earth, Bernice created a trench just deep enough to keep the foxes at bay, watching entranced as the dark soil fell between her fingers before patting it smoothly, restoring the patch to ground level.

She plucked a buttercup from the grass, surprised it survived past July. She would add the golden flower to her own Lammas offerings.

Hex sat motionless at the window, watching her every move.

Chapter 6

The next morning, Maggie arrived early. Bernice eagerly lifted her mail as she opened her front door. She sifted through it as both women walked into the lounge.

'Well?'

'Well what?'

'Is there another letter?'

'Nope. More bills.'

'I can't believe you sent the money. How much more are you going to pay out before you realise this is a scam?'

'But, Maggie, not many people know about my past. Whoever is writing this definitely knows something.'

'Bernice, you're clutching at thin air. Give it up before you drive us both crazy.'

Bernice paced the floor.

'No one would know about the baby unless they knew me back then, apart from you.' Bernice looked at Maggie.

'I haven't told a soul, I swear. Okay. We can rule your granddad out. Granny would have told you years ago if she wasn't so terrified of Granddad. So who else would know?'

'Dermott and Robbie. I wonder.'

'From what you've told me about them they are a pair of dimwits? Anyway, I thought you and Granny kept the pregnancy a secret? From what you've told me your old granddad wasn't likely to shout about it from the roof.'

'I know, but what if the boys noticed something, saw something, heard something?'

'What if? Why wait all this time? How would they know where you are? Why would they care?'

'The letters I wrote to Granny. Someone must have seen them. Maybe the boys are thinking I'm earning big bucks in the city.'

Maggie sat in silence for a moment. 'You any idea how mad

this all sounds?'

'I've got a feeling, Maggie. Please, please support me with this.'

'You can't keep forking out money you don't have. Ignore the letters. They'll keep coming and you'll never find out where he's buried. It's a hoax.'

'I'll get a bank loan.'

'Sure, "I need a loan to pay off a blackmailer." The bank manager will trip over himself to get to the safe.'

'It's not blackmail.'

'Of course it is. Please, Bernice, go to the police. If there is any truth in it they will help you.'

'No. Granny might get charged with aiding and abetting or something. I can't risk it.'

'I need to go. I want to catch a nap before Wredd gets up for his night shift.'

Maggie left Bernice engrossed in paperwork as she tried to juggle her finances.

Chapter 7

A busy train swept into Glasgow Central. People freshened up after the long journey. A young mother struggled to rise without disturbing her sleeping baby. The infant nestled in her arms, its face flushed beneath a woolly hat, as the train pulled towards its final platform for the day.

Two sailors stretched and yawned, ignoring an array of empty sandwich packets and beer cans strewn across the table in front of them. They each grabbed a canvas kit-bag and made their way along the narrow carriage.

Liam sat looking at his reflection in a darkened window, his elbow bent against the glass, thumb strumming his bottom lip. On the platform, a blonde girl caught his eye. She was around his age and walked with an air of confidence Liam never mastered. She pulled a leopard-print trolley bag behind her, pushed blonde curls under a hat with teddy bear ears and smiled. She carried on past the window without looking back. He watched and waited until most of the passengers left the train.

A man wearing a hi-vis waistcoat came on board, carrying a pile of plastic bin bags. He scooped debris from various tables shaking his head.

'No getting aff then?' he asked.

Liam nodded, pulled his rucksack down, and headed for an open door.

The station, brightly lit under glass panels, reminded Liam of his da's green house; one of his favourite places to be alone. The main throng of travellers were gone. Beyond the ticket barrier the young couple from the train hugged an older pair who fussed over the sleeping child. Liam stopped and watched the family reunion, wishing someone was there to greet his arrival.

A huge old-fashioned clock hung from the centre of the roof. His belly growled, reminding Liam of how long he had been on the road. The concourse was bordered by an array of small retail units, all closed for the night, except for one fast-food outlet. Liam headed towards it.

'Opening soon.' A tired-looking teenager was tying a bright apron around his waist.

'Are you closed now? Even a cold snack would do.'

'Anything ready?' the boy called to a figure behind the fryers.

'Coupla hash browns and a Gigaburger!'

Liam sat on a bench and wolfed it down with a bucket of cola. He plucked a scrap of paper from the pocket of his jeans. Two transport policemen approached him.

'You lost, son?'

'No. I'm going here.' He showed them the address.

'Not local, are you?'

'Just off the train.'

The officers exchanged glances.

'Got enough for a cab?'

A short discussion followed, after which it was decided Liam would experience his first visit to Glasgow by foot.

One of the policemen directed him out of the station onto Gordon Street. He turned left at the entrance to Central Hotel as advised, slightly taken aback at the sight of a bronzed fireman in his helmet and mask centre stage on the pavement. A feather boa hung around the neck of the statue; an empty foil carton sat at its feet, the contents spilled over a white plastic fork, lying congealed on the damp pavement.

Liam checked the street name, and smiling at the irony, headed up the hill of Hope Street. Tenement buildings linked along like a grey caterpillar taking a final stretch before sinking into its cocoon. A hemline of grubby shops skimmed the Victorian work of art.

Arriving in Sauchiehall Street, Liam was pleased to have reached his destination. He paused to admire tiled walls in the close entrance, bronze glazed with twisted moss-green trim. The tiles rose to a level of around five foot, above which the high walls stretched, skimmed with cream paint over smooth stone.

Liam rested his hand on the curve of a dark wooden bannister and looked upwards towards a wide spiralling stairway. Thick metal railings twisted beneath the wood. It was a long tiring day, the excitement and adrenalin wearing off as Liam climbed the stone steps to look for flat 1C. He lifted a rubber doormat squashed between a set of storm doors and found a key as promised. He trailed the musty hallway until he reached a scratched door with 1C scrawled on the post with black ink marker. His foot hit something solid. He recognised the cardboard box Ma packed for him and sent on a few days before. The box was damp, thick tape flapped around the half-open top. Liam turned the key. He gagged at the odour of the previous tenant, pushed the box with one foot into the room and slumped onto a chair. His search had begun.

A man loitered by the side of an old sandstone warehouse across from Bernice's flat. Cupping a cigarette in his hands he lit the tip and inhaled deeply. He turned the collar of his coat up against his ears and lowered the peak of his cap. He watched with curiosity as the bay window changed from darkness to light and finally a dim yellow glow. Checking his watch, he realised the streets would get busier soon with commuters. He took a final draw. With his sights still on the large bay window he crushed the cigarette butt under heavy boots, stuffed his hands in his pockets, and headed along the silent street.

Chapter 8

Maggie passed Wredd in the hallway.

'Decided to get up then? Thought it was me working the night shift.'

'My head was splitting, Wredd, you know how I get.'

'Oh yes, the old "I've got a headache" routine. I know exactly how you get.' He brushed past her and took up his Parker throne in the lounge. Flicking through TV channels, he muttered something Maggie couldn't quite catch.

She went into the bathroom, leaned over the washbasin and splashed cold water on her face. She rubbed at toothpaste streaks on the mirror, cursed her husband and gazed at her reflection. She stared, searching for the woman she used to be.

She thought of Bernice. No ties. No. Maggie wouldn't want to be in Bernice's shoes no matter which craft-crazy friend moulded the soft pumps to her feet. Maggie headed to the kitchen.

'You keeping an eye on the time?' Wredd called.

Maggie was pouring rich gravy over caramelised onions.

'Two ticks!' she called back. She creamed potatoes with Cornish butter and patted them into mounds to lie beside batons of carrot. Two peppered steaks sizzled under the grill.

The phone rang twice and stopped. Wredd laughed as Maggie slid the platters onto a tray.

'Forget it!' he called to her. 'Meeting Bob for a pint. I'll grab a takeaway on the road in.'

'But it's ready…'

He slammed the front door on his way out. Maggie looked at the food, and the array of pots and pans she would have to clean. Another shrill of the telephone interrupted her thoughts. She lifted it without thinking.

'He's already away,' she snapped.

'Who is away where, Mum?' The voice brought a smile to

Maggie's face.

'Oh it's you, Stacey, where are you?'

'I'm in town. Is it okay if I stay over later? I've got my key.'

'Of course it's okay, there's always a bed here for you. It's late now? Dad's gone for his night shift.'

'Mu-u-um. Going clubbing with the girls. Don't do that daft waiting up thing. You do enough with Dad.'

'Are you coming to drop off your stuff? I've got a lovely dinner…'

'I was going to come home first but got waylaid at the pub so I've left my bags there. Nick says we can pick them up tomorrow.'

'But I haven't seen you in weeks. How's the flat? Met anyone nice? How's the course going?'

'Fine. No and fine. Look, Mum, gotta go. Don't wake me early… Love you!'

Maggie wandered into the lounge. She glanced around the neat room; heavy curtains hung in swags and tails, a glass coffee table lay adorned with pristine magazines and a small vase of supermarket flowers.

She emptied the vase into a waste basket, annoyed at having to add her treat to the weekly grocery bill. She couldn't remember the last time Wredd bought her flowers.

Maggie poured two fingers of gin and filled the tumbler with tonic water. She picked up the telephone.

'Hi, Bernice. It's me. Maggie. Sorry about earlier. My head was splitting. Fancy coming over tonight? He's left early for work.'

'Sorry, babes, maybe if you'd phoned earlier. I've sort of settled in for the night.'

'Oh, no problem, I've loads to catch up on anyway. Thought you might fancy a chat about your family and stuff. I could come back round to yours?'

Bernice hesitated. 'Not tonight, Maggie. Maybe grab a curry one night after work?'

'Stacey's home.'

'There you go then. You two catch up with some mother-and-daughter bonding. How long is she staying?'

'She's not home yet. She is in Glasgow. Not sure if she's coming for the night or a couple of days.'

'Look. Why don't we all meet at Nick's tomorrow lunchtime, sample some of his great steak pie? How does that sound? Must fly. Bye.'

'I'll let you know. Depends on...'

Bernice hung up. Maggie scattered the magazines across the shiny table, dug her fingernails into the palms of her hands and took a deep breath.

Chapter 9

Shortly before dawn, a white van pulled into the lane beside Nick's bar. Nick answered a three-ring signal on his phone and stood outside his pub with the cellar doors open. The driver nodded and tipped his baseball cap in Nick's direction.

'Cold one this morning.'

'Sure is,' said Nick, looking beyond the man towards the main road. 'On your own today?'

The driver walked to the back of the van. 'Naw. The boys are still wrecked. Pulled them away from a couple of lumbers.' He un-padlocked the doors and two scruffy youths peered out. One stumbled to the pavement.

'Torture man. Torture. Loadsa drink in there.' The first to exit scratched his shaven head.

'You were warned it would be an early start. Get it unloaded sharpish.'

A second boy slid to sit onto the floor of the van, dirty trainers swinging from denim-clad legs like the pendulum of a broken clock.

'Any chance of a hair of the dug afore we start?' he asked.

'If you don't get a move on, you'll be in the pound, but naewhere near any dug. Now shift!' The driver shook his head and laughed. 'Calm doon, boys. It's early doors. We'll have this lot stashed away well afore opening.' He held out his hand as Nick counted a bundle of twenty-pound notes into it.

'You saw that Bernice one in a while?' the man asked. 'Bit of a go-er that one?'

'What do you mean?' Nick frowned. 'She's more of a flirt than anything else.'

'Got a soft spot for her have you? We met an old guy in a bar near the ferry. Lots to say about her and her mother. Bernadette O'Hanlon. Right?'

'Could be, but she hasn't set foot on the island in years, must be hundreds of O'Hanlons. I've always known her as Bernice. Who was the old guy?'

'An old lush by the looks of him. It was his accent we picked up on. Fiery temptress he called her. Never imagined he would know her like. Went off on a bit of a rant.'

'She's been away for years.'

'Oh, maybe just a blowhard. Said he knew her old man.' The driver scuffed the toe of his boot on the pavement.

'Can't be our Bernice then. Far as I know she never knew her father. Not even sure if her mother did.'

'Weird though. He described her to a tee. Seems she was the spit of her mother. Women of passion by all accounts.' The driver laughed. 'It's our Bernice is it?' He nudged Nick in the ribs. 'Like her mother in many ways.' He winked. 'Good gear this French plonk. Viva la France!' The driver laughed again. 'Viva la channel tunnel!'

Bernice spent the afternoon shopping. She caught her reflection in a shop window, oblivious to the man watching her from across the street. She scoured the mannequins and she calculated in her head, *If I skipped lunch for a week, kept the heating off and ate dinner at Maggie's I could buy that red number.* Her hand was on the door ready to push when she hesitated. Shoes? Sandals? It would be a shame to ruin the look with tatty old footwear, and she'd need a bag too. The man crossed over and stood behind her. Bernice stepped back and bumped into him, her eyes still on the display.

With her focus still on the dress she mumbled. 'Sorry, my fault.'

He didn't reply and she didn't expect him to. As she drooled outside the shop a little longer, the man was swallowed in a gaggle of schoolgirls and drifted away.

Chapter 10

On the island, Mrs MacEwan was eager to share the news. She opened her small shop early and hovered at the entrance, desperate to catch the attention of any of the villagers out and about.

'Morning, Mrs Mac.' Charlie rested his bicycle against the low stone wall that acted as a barrier between the shop and pavement.

'Hear the ambulance last night?'

'Nope.' He took off his cap and scratched his head. 'Nancy's bairn arrive early then?'

'No. T'was aul Mrs O' Hanlon.' Mrs MacEwan tapped her forehead, each of her shoulders and rested her hand on her chest. 'God rest her soul.'

'Sorry to hear about anyone passing.' Charlie squeezed past her. 'Kettle on?'

'It was a right hard life for her, the sowell.' Toast was buttered and sugar stirred. 'Her daughter drowned you know. Tragic. Then all that carry on with the young yin.'

'Bernadette? Sure, I remember the rumours. Shouldn't gossip about other people's misfortunes. Trouble can knock at anyone's door.'

Mrs McEwan folded her arms under her ample bosom and shook her head. 'Only showing an interest in me neighbours.'

A Post Office van drew up, the driver hurled a sack inside the door. 'One in the pot for me?'

Charlie started loading the letters and parcels onto the shop counter. 'Go on, Mrs Mac. I'll sort this lot.'

Mrs MacEwan sighed and scurried through to the back shop.

'What's with her face?'

'Aw the aul crow spreading bad news as usual.'

'Don't you go stealing my thunder, Charlie Roache.' Mrs McEwan thumped a mug of tea on the counter. She started to rummage through the mail. 'Ah. Mrs MacKay's daughter writing from the States, looks like young James is in trouble at school, Madge Pyper's hospital appointment, a martyr to her hip she is.'

The two men left her to her daily pleasure of patching together the lives of the villagers.

'Oh!' Mrs Mac Ewan caught her breath. 'Glasgow postmark.'

'So?'

'Well, aul Mrs O'Hanlon has gone now, maybe I should...' She poked a chubby finger under the seal.

'You certainly will not.' Charlie grabbed the envelope. 'You know old man O'Hanlon takes to do with her mail.'

'But he doesn't have the right. Never did have the right. You men, no shame.' Mrs MacEwan busied herself pulling elastic bands around piles of mail, sorting them into bundles. 'Go then. Go. Not even cold and you're still taking his side.' She flounced once more into the back shop.

'What's she all about?'

Charlie stuffed the bundles into his red satchel ready for the delivery. 'I promised the old man I would give any letters to him. Says the old dear gets too upset, what with Bernadette disappearing so suddenly.'

'Saw the curtains drawn as I passed. Thought it a bit odd.'

'Sure, last night it seems. Difficult enough time for them without her putting her tuppence worth in.' Charlie jerked a thumb toward the back door and called out. 'I'm away then. I'll pass on your condolences up at Worthing's farm.'

Mrs MacEwan stumbled past a recent delivery of potatoes. 'Don't you be passing anything of mine. I'm not one to gossip. I'll be paying my respects at the church.' She bent and rubbed at her ankle as it grazed the potato sack.

'I'll away too, missus.' As the van driver left an elderly customer was tying her dog up outside the shop.

'Ah, Henrietta,' Mrs McEwan forgot about her bruised ankle, 'did you hear the ambulance last night?' she asked, ushering the woman inside.

Chapter 11

Liam looked around the cramped room.

Ingrained layers of spillage of the previous occupants rendered the nylon carpet tacky beneath his bare feet. The sash window was splattered with pigeon droppings. A faded curtain dangled limply to the side of the frame like the victim of a hanging.

He rubbed his elbow across a smeared pane of glass and peered down into the street stubbing his toe on the cardboard box from home.

The box arrived before him. His poor old rucksack taking as much strain as it could, due to the cost of sending it all by carrier. Ma insisted everything in there was essential. The weather was dismal, the street deathly quiet. Most of the shops were shuttered against the elements, and the rampant crime Liam was warned about when he left the island.

A crack of light from a parked van's headlights caught Liam's attention, as a man trussed up in thick clothing threw bundles of newspapers towards a younger man in a shop doorway. Liam checked his watch. He unrolled his sleeping bag, made room on the sofa and sat back. He looked at the soggy duct tape on the box and decided to leave unpacking till later. He still felt hungry. Liam didn't have any intention of staying in Glasgow longer than necessary. Still, no harm in giving the place a bit of a clean, but first he needed caffeine.

The room was partitioned off at one end with a makeshift breakfast bar. He squeezed his slim frame behind a kitchen unit and faced the small sink. It was a single stainless steel bowl with an excuse for a drainer to the left. To the right was a kettle, so greasy Liam wondered whether potato chips were fried in it at some point. He lifted the lid and sniffed.

Hoping that boiling the water would kill off any germs Liam

reached into the pocket of his parka jacket and pulled out a tea bag.

He thought of the traditional breakfast he would have been served back home this fine Sunday morning: pork sausages and double-yoked egg, steaming hot tea; thick toasted soda bread would magically re-cover his plate as fast as he could eat it. Liam trembled and silently chastised himself for being such a homesick wimp.

This was his first day in the city. He'd thought of little else since his emotional conversation with Ma. Liam sighed. He would keep his promise. This was no ordinary journey and here he was sulking over a missed breakfast.

The overhead kitchen cupboards held nothing but more grime and the odd grain of rice. Liam emptied a plastic tumbler of its matted washing-up brush and splashed some hot water in, swishing the tea bag to puddle grey. Leaning back against the units he surveyed his surroundings. The foldaway sofa refused to unfold so he lay on top. The single-bar electric fire refused to glow. A thin candy-striped cotton sheet and a flattened pillow lay folded on a chair with two rough blankets Liam was sure must have been found during the last invasion of the army horse brigade; coarse as scouring pads. A low table sat in front of the sofa, its wooden surface scratched with the memories of his predecessor's lives. Cigarette burns and tumbler rings obliterated the varnish.

He knew he was to share a bathroom and prayed that a blonde mermaid lived next door.

Liam returned his attention to the box from home. He lifted a small frame and smiled at the photograph. A middle-aged woman stood straight and self-conscious in her Sunday best, arms folded shyly around the hand-knitted cardi she wore for church.

I'll make you proud, Ma, he thought, looking around for a suitable place to set up his shrine. A lopsided bookcase near the window seemed ideal. Liam set about emptying the box, and arranging the contents onto shelves. He placed the photo on top of the bookcase, alongside a small ceramic bowl with three joss sticks. He fumbled in the pocket of his jacket for matches and let the scent of lavender waft in thin smoky lines around the room. Ma's influence with her lotions and potions.

Lying back on the lumpy sofa, Liam dozed off.

The clatter of a milk van outside gave him the signal he needed to head across to the shop.

An elderly man stood behind the counter with gloved hands wrapped around a cracked mug of something hot and steamy. He coughed and spluttered with the hack of one who fed the fortunes of the tobacco barons.

'Aye aye.' The man nodded a welcome in Liam's direction. 'Help yourself, son.' The man's accent was in sharp contrast to his appearance. His head was swathed in a dark turban, one brown-skinned hand stopping a trailing grey beard from dipping into the mug.

Liam lifted a carton of milk from a stack inside the door. A younger man was busily piling them into a tall glass-fronted fridge. He looked like a younger version of the older man and wore jeans and a grey overall several sizes too big for him.

'Rolls not in yet. Couple left from yesterday if you want to toast them.' He pointed towards a wire-racked shelving unit. 'Half price.'

Liam laid the milk and rolls on the counter and went to look in the low fridge for some cheese. Sure enough, in the far corner sat a pile of perishables about to perish. The red stickers over the bar code a badge of temptation to a discerning shopper like himself.

Thanking the helpful duo, Liam paid and lingered outside the shop for a moment, scanning the postcard adverts for work. Nothing on offer but a baby's buggy and a set of dumbbells.

He decided to try the jobcentre next morning and headed

swiftly back to his new abode, blowing hot air on cold hands, the flimsy bag of shopping swinging from his arm.

Chapter 12

Stacey had been out on the town every night since she came home. In the early hours, party revellers headed home. The doorman at Zanzibar's nightclub watched as Stacey drifted from her friends. He stood statuesque in his black Crombie jacket, proud of the daily workouts at the gym used to bulked up his frame.

'Your pal said tae gie you this,' he said to Stacey as he pushed a piece of paper towards her. 'You went tae ma school?'

'Maybes aye. Maybes naw.' Stacey smiled. The doorman ushered her into the night.

'Cheerio, Big Bouncer!' She laughed, glancing briefly at the unfamiliar address on the paper.

Stacey tottered towards the West End, via a snack van, hoping to find a friend, a party, or as a last resort, a bench on which to perch until she savoured her weekly treat from the late-night takeaway. She wandered the streets turning corners aimlessly until she found herself outside a set of controlled entry doors at the foot of a tenement block.

Stacey screwed up her eyes and peered at the scrap she was clutching. She checked twice. It was the right address, but there were no lights on and no music. She wondered whether to wait and see if her friends would turn up, knowing all it would take was a smile from some half-baked lothario and without a moment's hesitation any one of them would head off on a quest for romance. A quick decision was needed. First some chips and cheese to ease her hunger pangs, then she'd seek shelter. She stuffed the French fries into her mouth and cowered on the stairs in front of the locked doors.

Stacey stretched into the phone box avoiding contact with the wet floor.

'City Cabz!' a voice squealed into her ear.

'Oh, hya. Can I have a taxi please?' Stacey asked, wiping her nose on her sleeve, as she struggled to balance her food and bag. 'Woman alone, so can you make it sharpish? I'm erh, in Sauchiehall Street, aye across frae Big Max's Snax van. Ten minutes? Make it five?'

She rested against the sandstone of the old tenement, her skull cushioned by a crown of blonde curls. Five minutes slipped towards ten as Stacey resisted the urge to sleep. The steps were cold and her bum cheeks were numb. She tried to read the time from her phone. It was getting cold now. Old man night swept along the narrow street looking for victims with his stark cold breath, blowing up empty crisp packets and other litter that skittered along the road in a desperate dance to escape the weather. Stacey squinted and watched the remnants of the evening perform their last waltz.

'Cheese 'n onion. Kebab. Fag packet.' She identified each with a snottery wave as they bowled past her on their merry bid towards freedom.

Wishing she'd chosen a heavier coat, Stacey stumbled momentarily to her feet and rubbed her numbing buttocks. Placing her handbag gently on the step, she lit a cigarette.

A man's brogue poked out of the shrubbery. Stacey was thankful there was no body attached to it. One shoe, alone in the dark. Stacey lifted the shoe, running cold curious fingers over the soft leather. Blowing smoke rings into the black velvet of the night calmed her. She repeated the operator's message:

'Green estate. Driver called Gerry. Green estate. Driver called Gerry.' She whispered the safety mantra lest any weirdo overheard and quickly spray-painted their old banger green, only to kerb crawl and shout a friendly, 'Hi there. Gerry it is,' from the rolled-down window of what could be a wagon to her doom. Distracted by her own imagination Stacey didn't hear him at first.

'Taxi for Stacey! Taxi, hen!'

Stuffing the shoe under her arm, she balanced a polystyrene box between her shoulder and chin. The smell of vinegar and cheese from the potato chips a familiar delight.

The voice belonged to the driver of a car wedged at the pavement. She thought she recognised the pink elephant dangling from his overhead mirror.

'And you might be who? Whom? Whit's yur name?' She breathed potently into the cab. It was a miserable night, and Gerry felt he'd soaked up enough Glasgow banter for one weekend.

'Prince Charmin. Cumoan you, get in, and dinnae stink oot ma cab wi yir grub.'

On closer inspection of her chauffer, Stacey sighed, content the driver was indeed safe to trust.

Sliding into the back of the cab, she held her cigarette packet high and smiled at the mirror above his balding head.

'Noo ye know better than tae ask.'

Stacey stuffed the packet back into her bag.

'Busy night?'

'Aye, hen, always is on a Friday. So where wiz it the night then? Where are yur cronies?'

'Och I could hiv stayed there awright but ah've goat responshibilities noo,' she slurred.

'Whit kinda responsibilities, hen?'

'Ma Mammy. Ma poor wee Mammy. A lassie needs tae help her Mammy.' She smiled the brightest smile and for a minute Gerry forgot how pissed off he was with his job.

'Mammee! Mammeee!' hiccupped Stacey. 'I'd walk a million miles fur wanny yir smiles weeeee Maamee!'

In his karaoke cab Gerry was entertained by a melody of tunes from Madonna to Max Bygraves before they reached their destination. Tapping stubby fingers on the steering wheel, he encouraged her to stay awake.

'Some chanter, hen. You would gie Carly Simon a run fur her

money nae bother.'

'Curley who?' She asked.

Gerry smiled at her youth. Curving into the dimly lit street, he parked by a patch of concrete outside of Maggie's home and waited until Stacey's silhouette vanished behind the frosted glass of the front door.

'Bloody wummin, roast yir hert.' Gerry laughed and released the handbrake.

As the car sliced through the darkness of a bitter cold night, he fumbled in the glove box for a lozenge and decided to call it a day.

'Switching aff fur the night,' he croaked into his radio. 'Aye the clubs are oot, don't expect any fares till the workers noo.'

An articulated lorry crossed lanes a bit too quickly, losing the green Volvo in its blind spot. Seconds later Gerry MacPhee discovered that his air bag was not serviced at the last M.O.T.

Chapter 13

The next morning, Maggie stirred a mug of coffee and flinched as a slice of bread popped up from the toaster.

'Good morning, mister heartache, let yourself in.'

The letterbox spat envelopes at her as she entered the hallway but she ignored them. Instead, she followed the trail of shoes, bag and clothing she knew would lead to a crumpled heap of humanity. Stacey's eyelids fluttered in distracted dreams. She lay on the bed, mouth open, snoring like an old fridge.

Stacey was cradling a man's shoe, a deep shade of purple with a black sheen. Maggie retrieved the leather comforter and placed it on the floor, remembering the last time her darling daughter brought a trophy home.

Only a few weeks earlier, Maggie opened her bedroom door to be faced with a four-foot plastic replica of an ice-cream cone. Ignoring Maggie's questions as to what possessed her to do such a thing, Stacey merely shrugged, smiled, and said, 'It wiz lonely.'

Maggie looked at the purple brogue, glad it was only a shoe this time. Where was the one-shoed man now? Perhaps fallen off some drunk, so at least they could be spared the whole return-of-lost-property dilemma.

Leaving Stacey to sleep off her hangover, Maggie phoned Wredd. She held the purple shoe in her hand, but chose not to mention it.

'Wredd, we need to talk.'

'I'm at my work! Go talk to Bernice.'

'Wredd, I know where you are, I'm not sure why though,' Maggie interrupted. 'I am really worried about things.'

'You can look after yourself. How is our darling daughter?'

'Stacey's part of the reason I've phoned. Listen, is there any chance you can come home early?'

'Not a snowball's, especially now you have interrupted my

shift with a phone call about nothing.'

'But, Wredd, it's important. You never said you were doing a double shift?'

'So? Says a lot about how much I enjoy being at home. What you got to tell me that can't wait?'

Maggie felt like a child begging for attention. 'Please stop with the wisecracks, Wredd. We need to talk. Please.'

'I have work to do. I thought I explained already?'

'Good for you.'

'I'm not listening, Maggie. Unless it's pillow talk you're after. I'm not interested in anything you have to say.'

Maggie held the phone away from her, reluctant to listen to her husband's babbling. Hanging it back on the stand, she wondered how long it would take for Wredd to realise the line was dead.

'Any paracetemol?' In the arch of the doorway, hair in solid clumps, slouched a vision of dishevelment. 'Think I might have flu.'

Accepting the two tablets offered, Stacey took a bottle of water from the fridge and shakily crawled back to bed.

'Nice to have you home!' Maggie called after her. 'I'm off to work.'

Chapter 14

Bernice curved Hex into her arms and ruffled his fur. She threw the duvet aside and stretched. As she pulled back the curtains, she looked down at the factory where Wredd worked. 'Murderers.' She flinched.

'Sma wee cuddlebums. You puffed out, son?' The cat escaped from her lap and followed her into the kitchen. Hex slowly strutted along the kitchen worktop before leaping down onto the tiled floor. Bernice grabbed a cloth from the sink and gave the worktop a quick skim. She started making breakfast and clicked the radio on. 'Better go into work today, keep the peace.'

'Local news team report a pile up on the M8 involving a truck and a mini-cab. It is thought a driver from local company City Cabz is recovering in the Southern General. More on this accident later.'

The grill on the old cooker rarely ignited independently. Bernice held a taper of kitchen roll towards the lit stove. As the flame caught, it shot out with a vicious lick the length of her hand.

She threw the fiery torch towards the sink and quickly pushed her sizzling digits under the mixer tap. The cold water temporarily anaesthetised the pain. She drew her hand back and the agony returned.

Bernice stood for a few minutes willing the pain to ease.

She thought of her Pagan beliefs, *Do no harm to others less it shall return to you threefold.*

'Oh, Hex, what have I done? I only wanted his cab to get a puncture.'

Two eggs bobbed under bubbles of boiling water in the pot forgotten by Bernice.

Bernice shivered and looked down at the back yard. The ground appeared undisturbed since her late-night ritual.

Tumbleweeds of litter fluttered over damp grass. She pushed her arms into the sleeves of her tunic and walked tentatively towards the front door. She stood listening for sound or movement on the stairway. Hex purred supportively as Bernice pressed the door handle down.

She rubbed at goose bumps on her arms and stepped quietly down the stairs.

Chapter 15

Maggie arrived late. 'It's her turn to open up. I might have known,' she mumbled.

The phone was ringing as Maggie unlocked the salon.

'Turn the alarm off,' she told the young girl beside her. As the salon junior punched in the code, Maggie shrugged her jacket off with one hand whilst pressing the receiver to her ear with the other.

The voice on the other end was familiar and gruff.

'Took your time answering didn't you? Salon opens at 8.30, it's now...' McIntosh paused, '...8.42. Got the figures for me?'

'Ah.' Maggie rustled some paperwork near the phone. 'Bernice must have taken the folder up to the flat to finish it off. Final tally.'

'Was she even at the salon yesterday?' McIntosh waited for a response.

'Of course.'

'And now?'

'The salon doesn't open till 9.00, but yes, staff are here for 8.30,' Maggie stalled.

'Bernice is there now is she?'

'Popped out for milk.' Maggie knew she sounded lame. She turned as a shadow crossed the window. McIntosh stood inside the doorway and dismissed the offer of tea from the junior.

'Oh, is it your car by the phone box?'

'She is a liability,' he rasped. 'It's your place as supervisor to mark her card. I think it's time to let her go.'

'But sales are up. The customers love Bernice.'

'When she appears. She lives above the shop for heaven's sake. She's unreliable.'

'But she has rights. Employment rights. She could sue; take you to an industrial tribunal.'

'Give her a month's notice.' McIntosh lit up a cigar and left.

'You're flogging a dead duck,' the salon junior sighed as McIntosh waddled back onto the street.

'He is such an arrogant arse of a man.'

'Bernice will get another job dead easy. She's magic.'

Maggie smiled. 'More magic than you think but as far as I know her landlord won't accept fairy dust. How will she pay her rent?'

'You're mad, you two.'

'We've been friends for so long, I can't do this to her.'

'You know what McIntosh is like, he won't budge now.'

'I know. His patience is wearing thinner than the cows lick on his balding head.'

'Mad. Totally mad.'

Bernice breezed into the salon.

'Never guess what I did this morning!' Bernice threw her handbag under the counter. 'Any chance of a coffee?'

Maggie shook her head. 'Where's the smoke coming from?' She stepped outside.

'Oh! What happened to your arm?' The junior pointed to the tea towel around Bernice's hand.

'It's my hand. Scalded it, daft accident.'

'With the kettle? Boiling water can be really painful.'

Bernice slapped a hand to her forehead. 'The bloody eggs!'

'Should I call the fire brigade?' Maggie crossed her path. 'Where you going now?'

'She's burnt her eggs.'

'Burnt her bloody boat.' Maggie sighed and called after Bernice. 'Make sure it's all turned off and get back here, you've a hot stone massage booked for half-ten.'

He could tell she was still a wild one, even from a distance. She never fooled him, never. Always rushing here and there. No sign of anyone else at her place. This was good. Best if they spent time alone. He watched her struggle to open the heavy sash window. Funny how she still scrunched her nose whilst concentrating, and that mane of hair, the way she pushed it off her face, oh so sexy. Old habits.

Smoke curled towards the street like a genie from a lamp. He turned up the car radio, titled his cap over his face and settled back to plan his next move.

Chapter 16

The only florist on the island was tucked behind the church hall.

'Never did like big displays at funerals. It's all about the sentiment. Now weddings, that's when you can go a bit extravagant, not that there's been much call for bouquets in your household, no offence like.' She curled pale blue ribbon as she spoke.

Dermott paid for the small wreath. 'You'll deliver to O'Brien's? She'll be lying in the chapel from Wednesday, so either way. Six o'clock mass if you want to pay your respects.'

She handed him a receipt and scribbled in a heavy leather diary. 'Don't you worry your head. The flowers will be right there when you need them.'

Dermott nodded to the customer behind him as he left.

'Shame,' the customer sighed. 'Poor aul sowell.'

The florist fastened the blue ribbon to a small cradle of white rosebuds.

'Would you look?' The florist turned the diary towards the customer.

'Would have thought lilies, or Viola Teardrops if money's an issue. The old farm has seen better days.'

The customer looked at the cradle display from various angles. 'You've done a grand job there.'

'Nope. He only wants bluebells. Wild flowers. I need to go pick them myself. Still, better profit for me. This okay for you? What they calling the wee mite?'

'William. Probably Billy for short.'

'Good traditional name. Give her my best.'

The customer held the floral arrangement as tenderly as a newborn and walked slowly to her car.

'Tea?' The florist's husband handed her a mug.

'Sure.' She blew on the surface. 'Billy eh? Might have known.

As orange as the walk itself her family.'

'Now love.'

'And bluebells! Who has a wreath of bluebells but Tinkerbelle herself? I tell you this shop will be the death of me.' She took a cautious sip of tea.

'Never blessed with a good family, Mrs O'Hanlon.'

'Right enough and the aul bastirt would be sooner spending his brass at the Pig and Bull.'

Chapter 17

Stacey leaned against the bus shelter reading a magazine. Her blonde curls tucked under the hat with the teddy bear ears.

Liam noticed her right away. He looked up at the timetable. 'Any idea when the next 62 is due?'

Stacey turned at the sound of his voice. 'Well, you can see from the timetable it'll be here in...' She ran a finger across a timetable on the wall of the shelter, '...Eight minutes.'

'Thanks.'

Stacey looked back at her magazine.

'Where you heading?'

'Meeting a friend.'

'Boyfriend?'

Stacey tucked the magazine into her bag and turned to face Liam. 'I am standing here minding my own business. Why don't you do the same?'

Liam blushed and rubbed the toe of his shoe on the pavement. 'Sorry, didn't mean to offend. Just saying, I've seen you around.'

'Where?'

'Here and there.'

'You stalking me, weirdo?' Stacey stood with her hands on her hips.

'Not at all. Nothing like stalking,' Liam stammered.

Stacey smiled. 'Calm down. It's a big city, especially when you're new here. You are new here right?'

'Been here a couple of days. Settling in though. Looking for work.'

'Why Glasgow?'

'I've family here.'

'Oh really, where?'

The bus drew up at the kerb. As they squeezed on, Stacey sat beside a frail old lady while across the aisle Liam was jammed beside a scruffy teenager with a huge Labrador.

Stacey leaned across the aisle, her knees touching Liam's. 'Try Nick's Bar in the precinct. Could do with a good-looking barman. Tell him you're a friend of Stacey's.'

Liam left two stops later waving aimlessly as the bus drove on, hoping Stacey would see the gesture.

Chapter 18

The island was colder than usual for the time of year. Sitting in the attic of the farmhouse, Dermott once again plucked the rusting biscuit tin from its hiding place. It was a big tin, one with a load of smaller ones inside. He bum-shuffled across the dusty floor to sit beneath the skylight. The tin was square, the image of a Regency lady and her suitor faded and scratched. Having set the old man up with a tab behind the local bar, Dermott was sure not to be disturbed.

'Are you not being disrespectful?' Robbie asked when told of Dermott's plans.

'I need to sort this family out,' Dermott replied. 'Your job is to keep the old man away from the house until I'm done.'

'I don't like this,' Robbie whimpered.

His older brother rested his hands on his shoulders and looked into Robbie's eyes. 'We owe her this.'

Leafing through the personal papers and trinkets, he found it strange Granny kept such a variety of useless things. Of course the legal certificates, insurance policies and the like were there in a folder. Dermott was more interested in what remained in the tin. He lifted a small plastic wrist band. Greyed with age it noted "Baby O'Hanlon-Male-". The date was worn off. He unfolded a parcel of tissue paper to find a tiny pair of hand-knitted blue bootees. He recognised her stitching. The woman he thought of as his mother. It was tradition in the village, Granny gifted a shawl to any newborn. Despite her ill health in later years she continued to produce exquisite smaller examples of her needlework. The finest soft wool woven like lace with shell edge trims.

Bundles of letters were tied with wool, all in date order.

'Neat as ever.' Dermott smiled as he slit open the first on the pile. "My dearest Bernadette."

Dermott was a strong man but reading Granny's words tested his strength. Thanks to the old man, himself and Robbie earned a reputation in the area. Not one Dermott was proud of. Now as he sat holding the old biscuit tin, he voiced his regret.

'Jeez, Granny, if only you'd told me.' Dermott thought back to his childhood.

When Dermott and Robbie were younger, Granny made sure she spent time with the two brothers; read to them, played board games and took them on long walks down by the sea. Dermott knew there were things best not discussed but wished now he had broached the subject of her daughter before. Not having children himself, Dermott could only imagine the suffering such a tragic loss must have caused.

"Yer reap what yer sow," the old man would say. "She was a bad yin and got her comeuppance. Brought shame on this family. I'll shed no tears for her. Now we're left with her bastirt runt to look out for, fecking Bernadette. She'll turn out a whore like her mither. As sure as the day is long."

Dermott stared at a fragile flower pressed between the pages of one of the letters. It brought back a long-buried memory.

Dermott must have been about ten years old at the time. He saw Granny from his bike one Sunday after church. He often skived off to go fly fishing.

"All yon heebie jeebie religion isn't for me," was Dermott's excuse to anyone who showed an interest.

Granny was down in the low woods and Dermott heading home on the high road. He was about to call out when curiosity held him back. He watched as she plucked a bunch of bluebells and hid them under a cover on her basket. He ducked as she looked this way and that way, patting the cover as she headed back towards the churchyard. Dermott slipped his bike behind a row of bracken and followed on foot, careful to stay out of sight.

Granny wandered to the far end of the cemetery and knelt by a small headstone. She wiped the stone with the corner of her apron and emptied a jar of dying flowers. Scooping up the jar and its contents she looked around her once more. Dermott ducked behind a tree. When he looked, Granny knelt before a vibrant display of blue-lilac blooms, her head bowed. She took the stopper from a vial and sprinkled beads of oil on the grave. Dermott felt uncomfortable and backtracked to reclaim his bicycle. He sensed not to speak of the journey he later discovered was a regular event.

Bernadette rarely came downstairs for half a year.

"She's not well," was the only explanation from Granny.

"Lazy, good-for-nothing runt." Granddad chewed at an old pipe.

Bernice was not missed by the men in the house. She was always a mystery to them with her singing and wanderings. Dermott caught an occasional glimpse on the few occasions she helped Granny hang out a wash, or carry wood from the barn.

"She's plumping up," Robbie said to Dermott one day.

"Maybes the old man is feeding her up like one of the turkeys. Maybes he'll take her to market and be shot of her."

Dermott remembered Bernadette being packed off to the city.

"Best for her," Granny explained. "This is no place for a gifted lass like Bernadette." The tears pooled in her eyes as she stayed loyal to her husband.

"Won't you miss her?" Robbie asked, thinking of the extra housework.

"I've you boys to look after. Be glad of the extra space." Granny scuttled off to put a batch of bread in the oven.

Dermott leafed through the biscuit tin some more; buttons, a novelty keyring, old photographs. A small leatherbound notebook rested at the bottom, a frayed gold ribbon hanging between the pages. He was torn between curiosity and respecting her privacy. He felt as though she somehow wanted him to read it, and so as the sky lightened above him, he settled with his back to the rafters and read Granny's diaries.

Chapter 19

The day dragged along. Maggie with her headaches and face tripping her. The flat still smelt of charcoal. Bernice opened the arched window in her bedroom. Hex curled around her ankles and purred. She bent to stroke him, cupping his face in her hands, before lifting him up. The cat folded neatly into the soft curves of her body as she planted small kisses on his head.

'Maggie Moaner is calling round later if you want to make yourself scarce.' Bernice stroked Hex's ears.

Bernice pulled a small basket from under her bed. The pile of leaves she collected earlier in the week, were dry and crisp.

Spreading the leaves before her she carefully drew a symbol on each one, for the regrets in her life that she wanted to release. Using golden ink, she scrawled a pound sign on one, a love-heart on the second and the third, a cradle. Bernice lit a white candle and lifted one leaf at a time. She invited the Goddess to take her problems from her. As she asked for strength with each, she crushed the leaves in her hands. They crumbled easily beneath her touch. She poured the fragments into a silk pouch which she would later empty into the sea to cast the problems from her life.

Taking a narrow white cord from the basket, she tied three knots in it to remind her of the regrets she sought to overcome.

Bernice tidied the basket away, snuffed out the candle and headed for a hot bath.

He watched the bathroom window steam up. He loosened his tie and rolled the car window down. He strained and wished for X-ray vision. Instead, he satisfied himself with her silhouette as she prepared to bathe. He wondered if she swam. Always liked the sea she did. He often watched her by the sea. She spent hours at the beach, but never let the water above her ankles. He imagined her gliding through the water like a sea nymph, her hair fanning across the water's surface.

Maggie let herself into Bernice's flat and found her curled in a ball on the sofa. 'Mission accomplished, Bernice. Re-scheduled your appointments for next week. Nudge up.'

'Oooh,' replied Bernice snuggling back into foetal position. 'A holiday for me then.'

'Look, I've told McIntosh you've burnt your hand, but can still take some clients. You come into work as normal, I'll try and cover for you, but you don't want to rock his boat right now.' Maggie muted the TV.

'Aw, Maggie, this one here is messing with her daughter's man and the daughter has been at it with her gran's man and now the other one is having a baby with her sister's man.'

'Who cares? Right! Up we get.' Maggie swiped a cushion at Bernice's head. Bernice avoided the blow and stretched with an exaggerated yawn, swinging her feet to the floor.

'I'll take some time off, get a line from the doctor.'

'No, Bernice, come to work. On time. Every day.'

'I have a clipped wing. I'm staying off.' Bernice hung her head to one side.

'I'll call back in the in the morning. We'll start the day with a good breakfast. Now, get a good sleep.'

* * *

'You got a new neighbour?' Maggie asked when she turned up the next morning.

'Not that I know of. Why?'

Bernice was tidying away her book of shadows. A short note fell from the shelf. It was her granny's handwriting "Don't drink and fly". Bernice smiled at the wise words and thought it no wonder things had gone haywire lately. She made a silent vow of sobriety, and tucked the note into the nearest book.

Maggie was still talking. 'Oh, a big guy in a suit charged past me on the stairs, must have been at hers on the third floor.'

'Must have been. Sure I had shoes on when I lay down last night.'

'Here you go, Dorothy.' Maggie handed over red sequined pumps.

'One click of these babies, and we're off to see the Wizard…'

'We'll get your hand seen to, then down to Nick's for a fry up.' Maggie threw Bernice's jacket towards her. 'Out.'

It was a short walk to the health centre.

'Good to blow away the cobwebs this,' Bernice grimaced.

'Sore?'

'Sore-ish.'

The burn was diagnosed as superficial, painful but superficial, and thanks to the early drop-in surgery the two friends were soon on their way towards the pub and a hearty breakfast.

Nick's Bar sat at the end of a row of small retail units.

'Looks like a carbuncle on a big toe, but I love this place.' Bernice held the door open for a young lad.

'There you go, curly.' She turned to Maggie. 'He's new.'

Liam brushed past her. Bernice watched a small white feather flutter from above and land on her shoulder. She looked back as Liam's slim figure disappeared behind the car park.

Nick's business had evolved over the years, from greasy spoon café to bar bistro, complete with UPVC conservatory extension. The previous night's lingering of bodies mixed with the greasy smell of frying bacon made things pretty hard to take so early in the day. Effie, the cleaner, cursed and swiped damp cloths over round tables. The stench of grubby mops a sharp flaunt to the health & hygiene certificates posted proudly behind the counter. Bernice kept her dark glasses on her nose as she took a short walk to the bar.

'Is it you, Madonna? No? It's Ms Zeta Jones? Tell me I'm right.' Nick, the owner of the urban oasis was already charged up to entertain his customers with a never-ending flow of banter.

'None of your cheek. Two of your Desperate Dan's, and a potta tea.' Bernice slid the sunglasses to perch on top of her head.

'Toast for me and make sure the tea is hot!' Maggie chipped in. 'Leave the butter on the side.'

'Sure. Anything for you two dolls,' Nick called back as he ripped the order from its pad and headed through the beaded curtains separating the bar from the kitchen.

'You look rough, Maggie.'

'Cheers, Bernice.'

'I'm only saying.'

'Well, don't say. I've got mirrors in my house you know.'

'Only trying to help, show an interest.'

Maggie shifted the napkin holder, rearranged the condiments.

Bernice tied her hair back with a scrunchie.

'Hair like a Clydesdale's hoof, my granny used to say.' Bernice smiled at Maggie and for a moment the tension eased.

The barmaid, Effie, silently slid a plate onto the table.

Bernice squeezed a generous dollop of brown sauce over the food.

'Who's fur toast?' Effie asked as she placed a smaller plate on the table and turned without waiting for an answer.

Bernice paused mid-chew and caught Maggie's gaze. They both laughed as the grease-stained figure disappeared back behind the bar.

'Think she failed the customer service exams.'

'Yes, sometimes people end up in the wrong job,' Maggie said pointedly.

'Fancy a walk up the Barras later?' Bernice ladled three heaped teaspoons of sugar into her mug.

The Barras were set in the east end of the city. A traders market since 1934 and renowned for hosting every type of band in its famous Barrowland Ballroom, which sat above the labyrinth of stalls, where you could purchase anything from antique bric-a-brac to pirate copy videos or batches of white terry towelling socks. Bernice spent a lot of time there, as comfortable in the musty alleyways of the market as she was in the darkened heart of the dance hall, watching her favourite bands play.

'No thanks. Why are you going there anyway?'

'There's a great wee stall with loads of cracking stuff. I was talking to the guy last week; he makes it all from recycled tyres. Soft as calfskin, but nobody dies. Bags, purses...' Bernice dabbed her potato scone at the egg yolk, creating swirls of yellow and brown on the plate.

'Maybe you should hold on to your money, Bernice. You never know what's around the corner. I mean, what if you lost your job or something?'

'Don't be daft, Maggie. Everybody loves me. I'm what keeps the place going.' She swiped a piece of toast across her plate, soaking up the last trace of sauce. 'Just what I needed. Sure you're not up for the Barras? The stuff is brilliant.'

'Bernice. McIntosh is talking about letting you go,' Maggie blurted, resting her gaze on the barely touched plate before her.

'If you don't want your toast I'll have it.' Bernice reached for the bread.

Maggie caught her un-bandaged hand in her own. 'Please, Bernice. Talk to me.'

'Oh, I was fed up there anyway,' Bernice quipped. Drawing her hand away she stood up abruptly. 'If you're sure you're not coming for a jaunt, I'll be fine on my own.'

Maggie grabbed Bernice's sleeve and pulled her back down.

Nick noticed the scuffle.

'I'm really worried about you, Bernice. You're still getting those letters aren't you?'

'I'm fine, Maggie. You worry about yourself.'

'You could lose the flat.'

'McIntosh doesn't own the flat. The landlord is sweet. Back in a minute.' Bernice walked away.

Nick sauntered over to the table. 'You on a mad diet or something?' he asked, clearing the plates but making no move to return them to the kitchen. 'Some guy's been in here talking about her.'

'What guy?'

'Some delivery driver. Seemed to think Bernice's old dear earned a bit of a reputation.'

'She barely knew her mother. Bring us some more tea and mind your own.'

'Must drive you crazy. Her being able to pack away the calories and not a pick on her. She was in fine form last night. Bit of a coincidence, the driver talking about her old dear's reputation then she shows up on the pull.'

'Bernice was here last night?'

Chapter 20

Alone in the restroom, Bernice recalled the events of the night before.

Nick's bar was already emptying as Bernice arrived.

"Last orders, you lot!"

Couples argued or smooched, dependant on their moods, with one or two lone souls cradling the dregs of their drinks, reluctant to face another night alone.

Bernice waved at Nick who slid a tall glass her way. He tapped his nose with his forefinger. Their signal the drink could be paid for later.

A sturdy stranger leant on the curve of the bar.

"Set him up a drink for me?"

"Bit of a bulldog, Bernice, you know what you're doing?"

"Any port in a storm." Bernice spotted the plastic ID tag, barely visible beneath the jacket of the drifter's crumpled suit. "Looks like a rep from the conference over the road."

"Come on, Bernice. Stay back, have a coffee with me." Nick slung a tea towel over his shoulder and continued clearing the bar.

Bernice mooched over to the man and soon locked in banal conversation. He followed her home like a lamb to the slaughter.

Bernice stared at her bedroom ceiling, ignoring the rocking gasps of the stranger sweating over her. She thought of a spider in the washbasin and smirked sourly at the imagery. The spider would be strutting its stuff, idly stretching each of its spindly legs. Gliding across the ceramic slope with not a care in the world, until some giant monster came along and turned the tap on. The flirtatious, confident spider would curl up in a ball and play dead allowing the force of the water to cushion its body, tightened up in protection against the inevitable. Sometimes the timing would be just right and the monster would be distracted long enough to allow the spider time to escape back to the garden, or under the floorboards. More often though, the game went on longer. The giant waiting until the terrified insect spread her limbs in one last frantic bid to reach safety then the heavy floods would set in.

The force pushing, pushing, until the spider, with no energy left to fight back, slid down the plughole into the slimy darkness of its fate.

That was sex for Bernice.

The handsome stranger from the pub turned into an ugly predator as she gradually sobered up. It was easier to play the spider game. If he was as drunk as her then the chances were he might lose consciousness first. Bernice mastered a way to escape in virtual silence, leaving the room like a hovercraft in slow motion, the monster slumbering heavily in intoxicated ignorance.

Bernice untangled their limbs and slowly slid from the bed. Curled up in a corner of her living room, she couldn't relax until she heard the familiar creak of her bed and bewildered coughing which seemed to be part of the signal morning had arrived. She once more adopted spider mode and curled tighter, listening for every move: the scrape of the bathroom door; the lid of the toilet whacking against the tank before a Shergar-proportion hiss of piss, as the previous night's ale was disposed of.

It was rare for any man to attempt to wake her in the morning; rarer still for one to leave a phone number. Nothing was ever stolen apart from another shred of her pride. Bernice pulled a pubic hair from her lower lip and gagged.

Once the coast was clear, she sprang into action. Never would so much bleach be used on so little space. With the price of bed linen in the Barras, a trip to the wheelie bin was often the case. Satisfied all trace was removed, Bernice clutched her coffee reward, and lit up a cigarette. Bernice didn't entertain condoms, challenging her body to replace the child she lost so many years before. She popped a couple of milk-thistle tablets. Then it was time to shower.

The bathroom smelled of the supermarket's special bleach offer, bought in nuclear-attack abundance and now no more. No amount of squeezing would get the last of the shower gel from the plastic tube. It hung on the shower tray as useful as an infertile sperm donor.

"Gawdsakes!" Bernice stepped onto the wet tiles losing her balance. She fell, legs akimbo, before a splitting thump brought her eye level with one of the biggest spiders known to man. The spider skated across the sudsy floor before scurrying through a crack in the skirting.

"Gallus." Bernice grabbed a fresh bottle of shower gel from the cupboard under the sink, and returned to the warmth of the spray. The jellied blobs slid over her skin creating a sheath of brief bubbles before being washed down the drain along with her tears.

Back in the bar Nick hovered at the table. 'What's going on, Maggie? I hate to see you like this. Wredd giving you a hard time again?'

Maggie waved him away. She walked to the restroom and knocked on the door of the only closed cubicle.

'You alright in there? Got you more tea but its stone cold.'

Bernice sat back against the door, her feet pushed against the base of the toilet bowl.

'Fine and dandy. I'll be out in a minute. Get me a bottle of water would you?'

Hearing Maggie's heels click back towards the bar, Bernice sighed in relief and hugged her knees to her chest.

'Don't let them get to you,' she muttered under her breath.

'Tell her I'm away,' Maggie told Nick.

Chapter 21

Bernice felt for the latest letter. It was folded into a neat square in her handbag. Maggie was right, why pay for information that might never be forthcoming. Bernice thought of another plan. With a quick wave in Nick's direction Bernice headed up town.

The building was down an alleyway, but Bernice supposed the location was the nature of the game.

A receptionist held the door open and Bernice settled in a chair, watching the young girl chew at chipped black nail polish. Bernice noticed the pock marks on her skin and wondered whether they were the result of chicken pox or bad piercings.

'You can go through now.'

The desk was old mahogany; solid with dark green leather inlay bordered by gold filigree faded with time and use. Bernice imagined some nutty professor, or historical novelist sitting for hours pouring their hearts into their work over the desk. Now it was lodged in Ferguson's poky backstreet office. A symbol of his egotism perhaps.

Ferguson scratched away on a notepad with his head bent, the glare from the street shining onto his bald pate.

Bernice wondered how long it would be before he deigned to acknowledge her presence as she continued with her scrutiny of the workstation. A modern phone with rows of lights and buttons sat on the desk. The distraction of a bright yellow pencil holder held her attention for a few seconds.

'Well! Good morning!' He looked up from the pad.

Ferguson rested his elbows on the desk, and coughed, with a brief whiff of the previous night's carbonara. He held his left hand towards her and let it sit in her palm like a cold kipper. No wedding ring, noted Bernice.

'Ferguson. And you are Mizz Hanlon.'

'Miss O'Hanlon. '

'Ah, may I call you Bernadette?'

'No. Miss O'Hanlon is fine.'

Bernice wondered whether the job transformed the man into this insipid hostile caricature, or whether through some gene deficiency this was his family inheritance.

There were no family photos on the desk. Experience taught Bernice most folks liked to keep an image of loved ones nearby. A reminder of their happy life outside work or a sign of guilt for putting in too many hours, justifying it by the implication they were doing it all for the family good.

Behind the yellow tub of pencils sat a small photo in a dark frame. Two Siamese cats peered out with slanted eyes. Bernice thought of Hex.

Ferguson picked at a hairy ear, looking distinctly bored as he shuffled through some paperwork.

'You know my rates?' Ferguson looked over the rim of his glasses.

'Of course.'

'Why me and not the police?'

'I want to be discreet. Don't want to rake up anything to cause harm to my family.'

Ferguson shuffled through the paperwork again. 'From what I see here, the only family of concern is your grandmother?'

'Correct. I don't want to cause any distress, I only want to find out where my son is buried.'

'Pardon me, but if you are so close to your grandmother, why has she not divulged this information to you way before now?'

'I have an awkward relationship with my granddad. I don't want him knowing about these enquiries.'

Ferguson leaned back in his chair and sucked the end of his pen. 'Been trying to give up smoking.' He stared at Bernice. 'You?' He offered her a pack of cigarettes.

'Not often and not now. Do you think you can help?'

'Mmm. It has been a number of years, and with no record of

the birth, or the death for that matter.' He sucked noisily on the pencil. 'Not a lot to go on is there? '

Bernice pulled the letters from her bag and spread them before Ferguson. He flicked through a few.

'You've not sent any money?'

Bernice flushed.

'Really? You are honestly so naïve?' Ferguson smirked. 'This proves nothing. In fact by all accounts, this child never existed.'

Bernice pushed the letters back into her bag and stood to leave.

'Please sit down. I didn't say it was impossible, more difficult and costly.' Ferguson kept his eyes on her.

'I realise it may be difficult but isn't that your job, to find missing persons?'

'From what you say, Miss Hanlon – O'Hanlon – this seems to have been some sort of miscarriage. You were very young, in pain, perhaps you are deluding yourself.' He reached across the desk and slapped his kipper hand over hers. 'There is no way I can look into this without digging up your family skeletons, no pun intended.'

Bernice stood and angrily pushed back the chair. 'Fine. You are not the only private investigator in the phone book.'

'Really? You have nothing to investigate. If what you say is true then both of your grandparents are liable to be charged with all sorts: concealing a birth, and a death, illegal burial of the remains. And the father? Sex with a minor? I really think you should put this behind you.'

'Thanks for your time.' Bernice barged past the receptionist.

Walking past the factory where Wredd worked, Bernice felt a sharp pain between her eyes. She hesitated and as she walked on by she felt another stab at her forehead. She rubbed her forehead and thought of Maggie. Could it be Wredd's feelings for his wife were somehow being transmitted through his work?

Chapter 22

Wredd enjoyed his job. He raised the electrode to the cow's head. 'Australia. Sydney is where I should be.' The animal faltered but stayed on its feet. 'Been a sportsman all my days.' Wredd pulled another shot.

As the carcass was moved to the next section, Wredd curled the wires around the rubber handle and hung the tool back on the rack. He wiped his brow. 'That's me for now, lads, another double shift under my belt.' He patted the shoulder of the man beside him and headed for the locker rooms.

'I wish he was in Australia.'

'Me too. Sick of hearing him bang on.'

'Failed the medical, didn't he?'

'Sure did. Pity that.'

'Aye, for us.'

Wredd stood under the showerhead letting lukewarm water trickle from a faulty valve. 'Ach, that'll dae,' he muttered angrily.

Once dressed, he joined his foreman outside the factory. The man was cupping a cigarette in his hand. He offered the packet to Wredd and let him take a light from his.

'November.'

'Aye. What about it?' Wredd asked.

'Nothing. Only saying. It's nearly November.'

'You been testing the equipment on yourself? Your brains fried.'

'Making conversation if it's okay with you.'

Wredd tossed his cigarette butt onto the road. 'It's been a long night. I owe you one.'

Wredd stuffed his hands into his pocket, turned up his jacket collar and headed off towards the twenty-four-hour garage. He recognised a white van parked alongside the air pumps and thumped the side door. It slid open.

'What the...?'

Wredd looked past the man's shoulder. 'Should be more careful you know, dossing out here with all this contraband.'

The driver laughed and invited Wredd to join him in the back of the van.

'Ach, got thrown oot ma digs again. Terry,' he pointed across to the garage shop, 'said I could crash out here for a couple of nights until I get rid of this lot.' The van was crammed at one end with boxes of beer and wine. A crumpled sleeping bag lay beside an empty pizza box.

The man flicked the ring pull on a can of lager and handed it to Wredd. They passed a good hour exchanging jokes and stories including how the old guy on the ferry talked about Bernice.

'Said some old dear would be the one to call if we wanted to get a message to anyone on the island. He was surprised when we told him she had lost her accent. Here, I got a number, somewhere.' The man rummaged in a small rucksack, and pulled out a piece of paper. 'Why you so interested?'

Wredd glanced at the number and stuffed in into his wallet. 'Oh, she's a friend of the missus. Maybe I can find out more about her family back home. She sort of lost touch with them all. A family reunion would be a nice Christmas present. Earn me some brownie points.'

The men exchanged a handshake before Wredd headed home.

* * *

Maggie was asleep when he slid in beside her. Or so he thought. She tensed and tried to keep her breath steady.

'You awake?' Wredd curved his arm around her. She threw back the duvet and rushed towards the bathroom.

'Jeez!' Wredd sat upright waiting for her to return.

'You haven't showered properly. I can smell sweat and blood.' She sprayed air freshener.

Wredd scratched a match against the headboard. 'Would it make a difference?'

'Oh please, don't start, Wredd. You're home late?' Maggie returned to bed.

'Yeah. Thought about what you said. Having a talk?' He rubbed his foot the length of her leg.

Maggie rolled away from him.

'Kitchen table's a mess. What's the pile of rubbish you're wasting time on?'

'Place-cards. For Stacey's birthday dinner.'

'There are only three of us and anyway, it's ages away.'

Maggie stiffened.

'Can't Warty Wilma make her own arrangements this year?'

'There will be four of us for the birthday dinner.' Maggie turned over her pillow and thumped it hard.

'She isn't family. Send her flying on her broomstick. Weirdo.'

'Four as always.'

'We'll see.' Wredd turned his back on her.

Chapter 23

Bernice lay still in the warm bath, conscious of her breathing. Slow, deep, contented breaths, at peace with her thoughts, the soft glow of scented candles making shadows dance on the tiled wall. She was conscious of heavy footsteps in the corridor outside her flat. The rhythmic thud reminded her of her granddad's heavy working boots on the path outside her grand-parent's house.

As a child Bernice often lay in the darkness of her room praying to the God she felt betrayed her childhood trust, to save Granny from yet another beating. One of Bernice's clearest childhood memories was coming round from a tooth extraction, desperately trying to outwit the dentist as she lay in the firm leather chair, her fingers bruised from where she struggled hitting her small hands on a metal canister linked to the chair, as the dentist counted backwards; 10, 9, 8... holding the mask in position over her tear-stained face, pressing firmly to make sure the gas invaded her system.

She woke in the chair, groggy and nauseous, choking on thick sticky blood in her mouth, her tongue lolling to the side. Granny dabbed at the gaping hole in her gums with cotton wool before pulling up the hood of her duffle coat and double looping the thick warm scarf around her mouth.

"To keep out the germs. Probably my fault, all those sugar and margarine butties must have rotted your baby teeth."

Bernice recalled the mornings when Granny's face was bloated from crying; a bruised lip, a grazed jaw. There weren't enough doors in the small cottage that could be walked into so often. Granny's shame was hiding from neighbours the truth of giving Granddad one pound too many from the housekeeping for beer money.

Granddad kept a selection of dried fruit lined along the dresser in their bedroom. Not currants and sultanas like Granny put in her dumplings, shrivelled up oranges each bearing a name and date etched in biro. Granddad said they represented friends and comrades he lost in the war. World War Two he said. Bernice wondered why the first war wasn't enough to the end the fighting but was always too scared to ask.

A large faded tobacco tin sat alongside the shrine. Inside, a batch of old medals and tangled ribbons fought for space.

"For bravery. Your auld granddad's a hero," Granny told her.

Bernice wasn't convinced.

"If you got medals for being a bully then he would have loads more."

"What was you saying, me darling"

"Nothing, Granny."

Bernice suspected him of stealing his dead soldier friends' trophies of war as they lay in the muddy trenches having given their lives for their country. He was probably hiding somewhere not even fighting at all, and that's how come he came home and they didn't.

The best tribute he could think of to honour their young lives was a row of rotting fruit? Bernice asked herself.

She pulled a fresh towel from the radiator and briskly rubbed herself down. With wet footsteps she went to pull the latch on her front door. Her toe caught on something on the floor. Another letter. She didn't need to read it to know what it said.

Chapter 24

Courtesy of the barman at the Pig and Bull, the old man lay in a drunken stupor, his black tie loose around his neck.

'What'll we do, Dermott?' Robbie pulled at his ear. 'Sure Liam's only been gone a day. Damn sin.'

'No worries. I'll track the boy down. He can't have got far.'

'But he says we have to go ahead.' Robbie pointed at the old man. 'With the funeral like. Stop messing and go ahead.'

'It would break Granny's heart not to have all the family there.'

'But he said.'

Dermott poured a tumbler of the old man's whisky and took a long gulp. 'He's not in charge any more, Robbie. Look at him. I'll take over from here.'

Robbie shuffled from one foot to the other as Dermott packed an overnight bag.

'I'll find the wee fella. You keep topping yir man up with the amber nectar.'

'What'll I tell him though? What'll I say?'

'He's out of it for a good few hours. I've an idea where the boy's headed for. I'll bring them home.'

'Them?'

'Get your head down, Robbie. Trust me.' Dermott turned at the sound of a car on the driveway. 'It'll be me cab. Now don't you go fretting. Get some sleep and keep him busy till I get back.'

Chapter 25

Maggie watched as McIntosh's car drew up outside the salon's front window.

'Your boss come into money?' asked a client. 'New car?'

Maggie looked out at the car, and squirmed as he hovered around the gleaming Mercedes rubbing an elbow over the bonnet before entering the salon.

'Stick some money in the meter would you?' McIntosh called to no one in particular. Maggie took a few coins from the pocket of her overall and nodded to the salon junior to carry out the request.

McIntosh flicked through the appointment book.

'Not a lot of activity is there?'

'Bernice's clients made up most of the regulars. They've been asking when she'll be back.'

'This is my business. Bernice doesn't have clients.'

'I'm sure a lot of them won't book with another therapist.'

'Anybody can slap oil on anybody,' he rasped. 'You've got the trainee.'

'Yes, but she's not a qualified therapist, doesn't have the experience.'

Maggie looked across at the enthusiastic young girl, as she rubbed vigorously at her client's skin like a celebrity chef preparing a new fish dish. The poor woman lay marinating like a slippery mackerel as she grabbed the corners of the treatment table with whitened knuckles, her flushed face jammed through the adjustable headrest.

'Not up for discussion.' McIntosh breathed heavily on his gold knuckle duster of a ring before rubbing it against the lapel of his suit. 'Bernice is history. I trusted you to keep things afloat, Maggie.'

Maggie felt a response rise in her throat, but thinking of the heap of final demands back home, held it back. Maggie was struggling to fill the appointment book. Bernice reclaimed many of her clients, who were only too happy to enjoy the treatments at reduced rates in Bernice's flat. It was above the salon where the most activity was taking place.

* * *

'He should never have let you go.'

'Cheers, Mrs Munro. How about I thread your eyebrows?'

'Maggie is nice enough, but she hasn't got your personality.'

'Maggie has a lot on her plate. Family stuff.'

'You never wanted kids yourself?'

Bernice paused. 'It wasn't in the stars for me.'

'Not seen you at Nick's for a while?'

'Too busy with work. I'm shattered by the end of the day. Loving it though.'

Clients were herded through the small hallway to her en-suite bedroom transformed into a mini treatment room. They never noticed the dust on the bottles in the wine rack and no one objected to Hex's occasional appearance. Bernice was enjoying her sobriety and happy focusing on her business.

* * *

Downstairs in the salon, Maggie wasn't prepared for the turn in conversation with McIntosh.

'Fresh start and all. We can wind it down, ready for a new venture.'

'It's nothing to do with Bernice is it? I mean…we are friends, but you know I never take clients outside of the salon. Never. '

'You know I have various business interests,' he told Maggie. 'It's nothing personal.'

'What about me? Do I fit in with your business interests?'

'Don't place any bulk orders for supplies.' McIntosh looked around the small salon. 'I'm letting you go, Maggie.'

Shocked, Maggie didn't reply.

'Penny for the guy, mister?' A young boy cocked his head around the open door. He was about nine years old with a cheeky grin, both front teeth chipped.

'Bit early for bonfires, son,' McIntosh replied. 'Still, never too early to get organised.'

'Which reminds me, Maggie. Where is the buildings insurance policy we got last year?'

Maggie pulled a box file from under the reception desk and placed it on the counter.

'Here!' McIntosh handed the surprised youngster a pile of pound coins. 'Now, you be careful when the time comes, fire can be dangerous. McIntosh gave a half-hearted wave as the boy stumbled over the stuffed dummy, his fist clenched tight around the coins. McIntosh watched the boy through the shop window.

Maggie followed his gaze. 'Please.' She touched his arm. 'Is there any way I can change your mind?'

McIntosh ignored her.

'Can't I manage the new place?'

'Look, Maggie, we both know you don't have any qualifications of a professional calibre.'

'I ran the salon for a long time. I have the experience.'

'Totally different quality of business.'

'Keeping the accounts is the same. I kept the accounts and the ordering and marketing…'

'It will be a fresh start all round.' McIntyre turned away from her, mumbling. 'Can't have a bulldog run a poodle parlour.'

'Sorry?'

'Nothing, sweetie. We'll give you a good send off. Here at the salon. Bring Stacey and Bernice. Time to hold out the olive branch.'

Maggie sniffled.

McIntosh shook his head. 'Get your man to look after you.' Tucking the box file under his arm he headed back to his car.

Chapter 26

'Hubble bubble, mine's a double.' Bernice slipped onto a bar stool.

'Thought you were back on the wagon?' Nick asked.

'Never been off it,' Bernice shrugged. 'Lemon tea, please. Iced'

'What you need is a good man in your life,'

'Like you, Nick?'

'You could do worse.'

'Oh believe me, I have.'

Bernice reached across the bar and clasped Nick's hand in her own. 'You know you are my safety net?'

Nick replied in an exaggerated voice wiping his hand over his brow. 'You mean tease, you use me like a plaything'

'Works for us both though.'

'Not sure it does anymore,'

'What do you mean?'

'I hate it when you go off with some random punter.'

'We're not dating, Nick.'

'I know, but it makes me uncomfortable.'

'Jealous? I am shocked,' Bernice mocked.

'I don't feel jealous. More protective, in a brotherly way.'

Bernice stirred the straw in her drink watching the ice melt. She speared a slice of lemon.

'I don't have a brother. I may have been brought up in the sticks but they don't all breed like cattle. Not even my toothless old banjo-playing grandpa,' Bernice giggled.

'What about those two? Declan and Bobby.'

'Dermott and Robbie. Funny you bring them up now. They were Granddad's toy soldiers. No relation.'

'What happened to their parents?

'Not sure they are human. Think they were defrosted from some evil eggs in the swamps.'

Nick cleaned the bar with a rag and moved to sit beside Bernice.

'Sure, my whole life has been one long nightmare filled with gremlins, tragedy and poison. Top me up?'

'It can't have been so bad.' Nick freshened her glass. 'You've turned out okay.'

'Gee thanks. Okay? Not fabulous or wonderful?'

'I do care about you, Bernice.' Nick raised his hands towards her. 'Yes, I did propose but I was drunk and you said no.'

Bernice nudged Nick's shoulder.

'Relax. It has always been a bit of fun between us. I know where your heart lies.'

'You do?'

'Qualify for a guide dog if I don't.'

Nick sighed. 'Missed my chance years ago.'

'She's never been happy with him.'

'Wredd's an arse, but she's too loyal to leave him.' Nick shook his head. 'I should have fought for her back then.'

'He'll push her too far, you'll see. Want me to give fate a hand?'

'Bernice, I don't believe for one minute in your jiggerey pokery, else why would you get in the states that you do?'

'I've lapsed a few times. Don't be so pious. At least I can say I tried. Can you?'

Wredd strolled into the bar looking tired and dishevelled. Bernice held two fingers like a cross in his direction.

'Evil spirit be gone!'

Nick moved back behind the bar and walked to the end where Wredd stood. He placed a beer mat down. 'What you having?'

'Usual. Who's she cursing now?'

'Ach, just messing.'

'Tramp.'

'Aw come on, you're being a bit harsh.'

'Gypsies, tramps and thieves, that's the islanders.'

Bernice sidled up beside Wredd. 'No. That's a song by Cher.' She started singing. 'Gypseeeees. Traaamps and Theeeves.'

'Can't a man have a quiet pint?' Wredd stormed off to sit in one of the booths.

'A-R-S-E-H-O-L-E,' Nick mouthed to Bernice.

'Indeed.' Bernice crossed over to join Wredd.

'Bad day with the ponies?' She slid into the booth.

Wredd leaned across the table so close to her Bernice could smell his sweat.

'You know you want me. Stop playing games.'

'Yeh, I want you, away from Maggie. Far far away.'

'It's never going to happen. Give it up, Bernice, whadya say we go back to your place?'

A spider appeared and crawled onto the table top. Wredd caught Bernice following its journey across the Formica. He quickly pressed the beer mat hard over the insect and banged his tumbler down heavily a few times.

'You are an evil moron.' Bernice stood to leave.

Wredd grabbed her wrist. 'I'm watching you. Every move you make, every breath you take.' He paused and finished the dregs of his beer. 'Another song for you. Come on now let's go back to yours and make sweet music.'

Bernice dug her fingernails into the back of his hand. Wredd loosened his grip.

'You're like a wee boy who has just discovered his penis. Go play in the traffic.'

Bernice hurried out the door.

'Mind if I kip down here a while?' Wredd leant on the bar.

Nick shrugged. 'A while?'

'Maggie's lost the plot.'

'How come?'

'She's letting that plank McIntyre throw a leaving party for her and expects me to go. Me? Amongst all those nippy wummin? And him? I'd deck him.'

'Maybe she's looking for support, but hey,' Nick raised his palms towards Wredd, 'I'm only the barman.'

'Maggie's too busy supporting barmy Bernice.' Wredd pulled the phone number from the van driver out of his pocket and grinned. 'Same again, with a whisky chaser.' Wredd tapped his fingers on the bar top. 'It'll give her a fright. She'll be begging me to come home.'

'A few days then. I don't want caught in the middle of any matrimonials.' Nick served the drink.

* * *

The short walk home calmed Bernice slightly. Her hand trembled as she unlocked her front door. Once inside she double-locked the mortice and slid the chain on. Hex sauntered towards her.

'I wish he'd gone to Australia. On his own.'

She flicked some music on and drew the curtains closed. The phone rang.

'Hello?'

'Hi. It's Nick. Everything okay?'

'Sure. Allergic to arse.' Bernice laughed. 'Buttock Brains still propping up the bar?'

'Looks like he's in for a session. Sure you're okay?'

'I'm fine. You go serve him some arsenic.' Bernice laughed again. 'Serve the arse, Nick.' She hung up.

Bernice turned to Hex. 'Casting spells can be a tricky business when your heart tells you only to do good.' Hex licked his paws.

'But, if getting rid of Wredd does Maggie good, it can't be bad. Can it?'

Hex lifted his back leg and groomed his nether regions.

'Show off.' Bernice turned away. 'Now,' she said, pulling various books from the shelf. 'Nothing too drastic but needs to be strong enough to get him out of Maggie's life. Maybe take McIntosh with him.'

She gathered fresh herbs from her window planter and began to grind them with a mortar and pestle, Wredd's image firmly in her head.

'Gypsies, tramps and thieves...' she sang as she worked.

Chapter 27

Wredd answered when Bernice called.

'She's busy. Busy trying to find work now you've pulled the carpet...'

'I was sacked first, remember?'

'Quite rightly. You're a waste of space.'

'Not what you said last time we spoke.'

'I was bullshitting you.'

'Really?' Bernice laughed and hung up the phone.

'Oh, Hex. He is a slimy moron.' She punched a cushion. 'Maggie deserves so much better.'

Hex curled into a ball and closed his eyes.

Bernice normally practiced as a solitary witch. She occasionally considered contacting a coven to share the sabbats with her. Her recent visits to the moot only convinced her she was better alone. Maggie didn't share her beliefs but was a great emotional support.

Bernice made preparations for the ritual she planned after sunset. She would light a black candle to end the year, and a white one to start the new year. Granny's gift on her tenth birthday was a pouch of runes she would use for her divination. The Goddess would surely forgive Bernice's past misdemeanours and give her the wisdom she sought to help her through the dark times she faced.

This was the end of Bernice's year, the one day of the year when the veil between the living and the dead was at its sheerest. It was usual for witches to lay an extra place at their feast, to welcome loving spirits back into their lives, but only if the spirits chose to join them. Bernice was not sure whether her son's spirit could find his way to her. She lit a candle in the window of her living room to guide him, hoping that he would.

A small white feather fell from the curtains as Bernice

fastened them safely away from the flame.

The man watched her pull the curtains aside. Her face was out of focus in the dimly lit room. Hex sat on the window ledge and stared directly at him. Hex caught the man's gaze and held it. The man shifted from foot to foot cursing under his breath. He bent his head against the wind and hurried away.

Chapter 28

Maggie stopped off at the mini market on her way home.

'Monkey nuts? Skeleton lollies?' a young girl asked as she rung up Maggie's groceries.

'I don't have any young kids.'

'Trick or treaters?'

Maggie sighed. 'Go on then.'

With her mind distracted, she loaded her basket with treats, shocked at the final tally when the numbers popped up on screen. Still, it was nice to be nice and she was sure Bernice would appreciate the gesture.

Loaded down with shopping bags, Maggie stopped off at Nick's.

A six-foot-two bunny rabbit beckoned her closer to the bar.

'Got any carrots?' it asked.

'Sure, Nick, but they're all frozen.' She dumped her bags and slid onto a bar stool. The rabbit hopped playfully from one pump to the next, before making a sweeping gesture with a giant paw towards the well-stocked gantry.

'What's your poison?'

'Coke...' Maggie smiled. 'Oh, stuff the headache, I need some Dutch courage. I'll have a large gin and tonic, easy on the tonic.'

'Ice and a slice?'

Maggie nodded. Nick shot two fingers of gin into a tall tumbler, and topped it up with tonic water. He secured a twist of lemon to the rim and placed it on a mat before her.

'On the house. You look as though you need it. You should see a doctor about those headaches, Maggie.'

'This Halloween lark has gone to your head,' Maggie said, changing the subject and taking a long grateful sip.

'Don't be daft. Got to keep my customers sweet. Talking of which – where is the sweet Ber-na-dette.'

'Don't let her hear you call her Bernadette, Nick. It's a sore subject.'

'I'm all ears,' he smiled, pouring himself a large soda water. 'Dish the dirt.'

'You two aren't an item anymore. Or have you forgotten?'

'Showing a friendly interest.'

'Really.'

Nick took off the rabbit head and placed it on the bar. 'I want to help.' He pulled a stool close to Maggie and wriggled to get comfortable, his bob-tail being a bit on the large side. He leaned on one elbow with his hand under his chin. A furry paw hung from a cord in his sleeve. It dangled dangerously close to Maggie's drink.

'Watch it, Bugsy. Nearly caused an accident there.'

Together, they lifted their glasses.

'Cheers, my dear.' The tumblers made a pleasant clinking sound, the rattle of ice leaving a lull in the conversation.

'Bernice is fine, Nick. It's me who is having problems.' Maggie blushed. She wasn't sure whether it was the start of another headache or the quick shot of gin, but unbuttoned her jacket anyway.

'Tell me all about it. If you want to? Rabbits are lucky you know.' Nick smiled.

'Nothing to tell, same old same old. Look, I'm only having the one,' she insisted.

Nick motioned to Effie to top up Maggie's glass. 'Nonsense. G and T and my usual.'

'A Coke,' Maggie insisted.

Nick leaned closer to Maggie. 'Having a bit of a shindig later if you fancy it? Maybe bring Bernice out of the shell she's been hiding in. Don't think my profits can take much more of her abstinence.'

'I'm hoping to catch up with her tonight, Nick, but I can't promise anything.' Maggie lifted her bag and slipped off the stool. 'I think she's saving for a trip away.'

Nick watched as Maggie leant against the wall of the phone booth.

'Hya. It's Mum. Listen, will you invite Bernice over tonight? It might sound better coming from you.' Maggie took a last sip at her drink. 'Hoped we could break the ice a bit… I know, I know, but somebody has to make the first move, and I've got toffee apples!'

Chapter 29

Later, as Liam polished the optics, looking in the mirrored wall behind, the pub door opened. Bernice rushed in dripping wet and struggling with an umbrella.

Stacey sat in a corner booth sipping a lemonade and lime.

'Took you on then?' Stacey called to Liam.

He joined her. 'Yeh. I was mortified though, lost one my best shoes during the flit. Had to interview in these old trainers.'

'Was it a leather brogue? Kinda purple?'

'Aubergine. How did you guess that?'

'Liam!' Nick called from the kitchen. Distracted, Liam went inside.

'It's Baltic out there.' Bernice shook the umbrella in Stacey's direction.

Stacey strained to see what was going on in the kitchen. Bernice shook the brolly over Stacey's head.

'Chuck it!'

'A wee bit of water never hurt anybody,' Bernice sniffed. 'Not made of icing sugar are you?' She shrugged off her damp coat.

'No. I wanted to give you the business cards.'

'You could have got Maggie to drop them in at the flat.'

'Did you bring the other cards, for my fortune?'

'Of course, in my bag. So what's up, Stacey?'

'Nothing. Nothing at all. I wanted to see you.'

'Well, here I am.' Bernice shuffled a pack of Tarot cards and spread them on the table. 'Loosen them up a bit.'

Stacey was distracted by shadows near the window. The rain battered off the glass as a young girl struggled past, one hand on a pushchair, the other dragging a reluctant toddler behind her. An older couple huddled in a bus shelter, the woman fighting with a tangled umbrella as the man pulled the collar of his jacket higher, his neck shrinking into the warmth. As the woman continued her struggle, he intermittently poked his wrinkled face from beneath his cap to mutter something to her.

'Take a deck at tortoise man!' Stacey laughed.

Bernice glanced across at the squabbling couple, and laughed with her. The man took the damaged brolly and rubbed the woman's arm affectionately as he placed his cap on her head.

'Awwww. At least she's got a man.' Bernice sighed. 'Get a bacon roll on order; I'm off to speak to Nick'.

Nick was bent over a crate of small glass bottles behind the bar.

Bernice leaned across. 'Full moon. Full moon. I see a full moon.'

'Aye very funny, Bernice. What are you after?' Nick straightened up adjusting the waistband of his bunny suit, glad of the interruption.

'I wondered, have you thought any more about what I asked you?'

'If it involves money, like me lending it to you, then no. No. No. The answer is no.'

'I want to put some business cards around the tables, Nick. What with me being an entrepreneur like yourself '

Nick thought of his clientele.

'Don't think you'll get much business, but go ahead, Bernice, if it shuts you up. Now let me get back to shelving these mixers, would you?'

'Cheers, wee fella.' Bernice caught a glimpse of Liam through the kitchen porthole. 'New barman?'

'Trial run. Now, go away.'

Bernice sat back at the table with Stacey, happy to see the double-dose bacon roll on the table and pleased to have another outlet for her business cards.

'These are great, more than great.' In between mouthfuls of Ayrshire's finest, Bernice admired the small cards.

'McIntosh will go mad if he gets to hear.'

'Been mad for years, sweet pea. It's his fault any-roads, cutting me out of the picture. I've built up a healthy list of customers. Not my fault if he rips them off at the salon. Shame about your mum. She deserves better, in many aspects of her life.'

Stacey kept quiet.

'I was thinking of some special offers for November. Get the Cabbage Patch Dolls of the neighbourhood Barbied up ready for the party season.'

'Bernice, you need to use a bit more tact. These wummin pay yir rent.'

'I know, I know, but honestly, some of them! Candidates for the Ugly Bug ball?'

'Bernice! I'm shocked at you. What happened to the inner beauty you are always on about?'

'Only joking. I'll be good. It's a bit heavy going, pummelling thunder thighs, and trying not to laugh when they spill out their gear for the weekends, bingo wings a flapping at one end, camel toes straining at the other. Because something is made in a size twenty-two, doesn't mean it looks good. You're right though, some of them have such a hard time of it. Good on them for getting out there.'

Bernice smoothed a hand over her slim thighs, pulled her stomach tighter, and straightened her shoulders.

'Bernice?'

'Bernice is my name.' She flicked through the business cards. 'Love the logo.'

'Going solo has been great for you.'

'More scope to expand from beauty treatments to crystal healing and herbal therapies.' She fingered the cards seductively and smiled. 'Classy. Bit like me.'

'Mum wants you over tonight.'

'How many did you print off? How much for leaflets? I can see this painted on the side of a minivan. Blacked-out windows like a tiny stretched limo. Posh or what?'

'Bernice. Did you hear me? Mum wants you to come over tonight.'

Bernice sighed and flopped back in the chair. 'What Mummy wants, Mummy gets, right?'

'Look, don't shoot the messenger. Please come over. For my sake. I can't be around all the time.'

'I get so fed up sometimes.' Bernice looked straight at her. 'Your mum doesn't get it. I'd love a smart cookie like you to care about me.'

'Oh, Bernice, I love you like a second mum, you know I do.'

'Second mum. Second best.'

'Mum told me about the letters, the baby you lost, Bernice, but it was a long time ago.'

'I didn't lose him, Stacey. He was taken away from me. Gone to be an angel in Heaven, according to your mum.' Bernice continued, 'Trouble is…I never got a chance to hold him in this world. What's to say I will in the next? It's not just the baby. It's everything. I feel I should have fought harder to stay with Granny, you know? She was the only one who cared. These letters might be a hoax, but it's given me hope.'

'You've lived a hard life. For you to lose your mum so tragically and so young. Must have been scary.'

'Mum's spirit is always with me. I dream about her sometimes and I get the feeling she's looking after the wee barra for me.'

'Mum needs you, Bernice. She's too proud to beg.'

'Told me she never told anyone about the baby. Who else knows?'

'Oh, Bernice, I dragged it out of her, she only told me recently because she's worried you're heading for a big disappointment, not to mention bankruptcy.'

'Suppose she means well.'

'You're a good person, Bernice.' Stacey wiped her nose with a sleeve. 'A bit dippy, but a good person.'

Bernice smiled, pushed back her chair and picked up a bundle of the business cards.

'Right enough, Stacey, too good for this crazy world. Your mum doesn't get it. Anyway, moping about won't get the rent paid. There…' She pushed a half-eaten bacon roll towards Stacey. 'Tell your mum I'll be round about eight. You finish off the food. I'll need to keep a check on myself. Nobody wants to get their teeth polished by a gummy dentist, if you catch my drift.'

'My reading?' asked Stacey.

'Do it tonight, after your mum finishes grovelling for forgiveness.' Bernice laughed. 'I'll away then.' Bernice left Stacey to finish off her leftovers.

Seconds later, Liam returned with a palette of clean glasses. He lifted one of the business cards.

'She's my auntie!' Stacey called. 'Could get you a discount. Back, sack and crack. Once your bum fluff starts to grow.'

Liam blushed like a bashful schoolboy.

Chapter 30

Wredd was noisily packing a suitcase in their bedroom. Maggie leaned on the door jamb.

'What are you talking about? Going where?'

'Leaving. You. This fucked-up triangle with Bernice. See how you cope without me.'

Maggie felt guilty relief. 'For how long?'

'As long as it takes you to see her for what she is.'

'I don't understand, Wredd, Bernice and I have been friends a long time, why now? Why does she bother you so much now?'

Wredd thought of his recent conversations with Bernice and growled. He zipped the suitcase shut and dumped it onto the floor.

Maggie stood in silence as he threw his door keys onto the side table, knocking over the frame and clock. She stepped forwards.

'Leave it!' Wredd shouted. 'Broken, like our farce of a marriage.' He pushed past her into the hallway.

Maggie heard the front door slam as she scooped up the broken glass. A sliver nicked her finger and she sat in silence watching the blood drip onto the broken frame.

* * *

Wredd spread himself out on Nick's sofa, his belongings scattered around the small back room.

'A week at most,' Nick reminded Wredd.

The arrangement was for Maggie's sake. Nick would keep an eye on Wredd until he calmed down.

'What do you think of our Bernice?' Wredd asked.

'There's more to Bernice...'

'...Than meets the eye. You bet there is and I'm the very man to find out what her dirty little secrets are.'

'Why all the interest? You should know better than to try and come between a woman and her friends.'

'She's coming between me and my woman, Nick. Maggie and I would be fine if it wasn't for her. Interfering bitch.'

'Would you really?'

'What?'

'Would you and Maggie be fine? You don't seem to put much effort in, Wredd, not from where I'm standing.'

'Oh you think so! So where you're standing, behind the bar of a grotty pub in a grotty estate, you can see the world and all its woes. Never been married have you, Nick? Oh no, you prey on vulnerable wives who come in for a shoulder to cry on when bad hubby doesn't play ball.'

'Oh, get a grip, Wredd. Take a look at yourself.'

'No. I'm taking a look at you, and guess what? It's all falling into place now. You and Maggie. Not enough you've messed with Bernice and God knows who else, but got Maggie in your sights too.' Wredd got to his feet.

Nick backed off towards the door. 'Listen, caveman, I don't know what you're on but Maggie and I are friends and no more. You ought to give yourself a good talking to. Now, I'm busy.'

Nick went through to the bar. Wredd paced the floor and lit a cigarette. He looked at the phone number from the van driver, lifted the phone and dialled, tapping his foot as he waited for the connection. Engaged.

Chapter 31

Bernice was browsing through the anonymous letters. Perhaps Maggie was right. Having worked her butt off since she went solo, she was prudently saving to go back to the islands and rescue Granny. She was stronger now and the villagers couldn't hold their own water. Soon she would know the truth about the burial. *Granddad will be decrepit now,* she thought, *don't expect much resistance from him.*

A large brown envelope slipped through the letter-box.

'HMRC?'

Hex flipped his tail into a question mark and kept his eyes closed.

'Curiouser and curiouser,' Bernice said as she ripped the seal. The letters blurred as she tried to scan the two-page document.

"Advised by a concerned citizen... Using residential premises, for business purposes... Health and Safety... Assets frozen until further enquiries."

She squashed the letter into a ball and lifted her phone.

'That scrotum has dobbed me in!'

Maggie held the phone away from dripping hair, streaks of dye slithering down her neck. Fumbling with a plastic shower cap, she tried to restrain the wayward locks, whilst balancing the phone between her hunched shoulder and left ear. 'Who did what?'

Bernice launched into a tirade of short, shrieking, rants.

'Can I phone you back in five?' Maggie hung up and unblocked some soapy gunge from her ear, dropping the towel from her shoulders.

Bernice stuffed a fist into her mouth, bit down hard and smoothed the letter flat. HMRC. Circling paragraphs with red pen she planned how to beat the Judas McIntosh to a pulp with the olive branch she begrudgingly held out when she got the invite to Maggie's leaving do.

Bernice chose to ease her temper in her own way, and was soon submerged in a bath full of lavender salts and froth. As she slid down to touch the bubbles with her nose, her hair floated on the water's surface like seaweed around a mermaid. Bernice sat up and squeezed the ends. She smoothed her hands over her tummy, inhaled a long deep breath, and exhaled to make her belly-button stick out.

She couldn't remember much about his birth: a faint recollection of pain slicing through her body, a lot of commotion from Granddad, the room fading to black. Bernice woke to an empty cradle and Granny staring out of the window, tears staining her cheeks.

She took the angelite crystal and held it tightly in her hand, willing herself to face up to the pain of the past.

Barely past her fifteenth birthday, Bernice discovered there was more to life than dancing reels, climbing trees and her other favourite childhood pastimes.

Tam McShane was a local bus driver. A heavyset man with a thick neck, fingers gnarled with toiling the fields for years. He had succumbed to the tourist trade and given up his plough for life behind the wheel, ferrying gullible travellers around the countryside as he peppered factual statements with folklore and myths. Not many would question his tongue-in-cheek repertoire. His reputation made sure they didn't.

Always the joker, Tam shared a pint with any brave enough to stand in his company. For when the Devil's nectar passed his lips, he transformed from gentle giant to raging bull. On one such night it was Bernice's misfortune to bump into him as he staggered home from the Pig and Bull, much the worse for wear. A few tourists strayed into the bar and enjoying the banter, set up a line of drinks for their newfound friend, little knowing the effect this would have. As Tam knocked them back, his features changed, his smile turned into a leer, his fists clenched tightly. His new friends, oblivious to the transformation, continued to joke with him. Tam's sense of humour shrunk a little more with each shot of malt. His friendliness towards one of the women in the group grew to desire. As the liquid burned in his belly, the bulge in his pants grew hard. He grabbed her arm; the young woman flinched and tried to brush him off.

"Enough, pal." Dougie witnessed the whole thing from his focal point behind the bar.

"City whore!" Tam spat. The group of tourists fell silent as he turned a reddening face towards Dougie.

"Don't pal me, Dougie. This one has been asking for it all night." Leaning closer to the girl, he fumed into her terrified face. "And you are going to get a bit more than you asked for."

Dougie signalled to three regulars at the far end of the bar. Granddad and his two pets, Robbie and Dermott laughingly obliged.

In a short time, Tam found himself headfirst out of the swing doors, and before long he was splodging through the rain like a homing missile towards his car.

Bernice was on her way home from dance practice. Feeling pleased with herself, she clutched a certificate under her raincoat and pulled a medal once more from her pocket.

Grade 1 Silver, the words glowed under the streetlight as Bernice fought against the driving rain, high as a kite on life. The car swerved towards her before screeching to an abrupt halt. Recognising her granddad's friend, she accepted his offer of a lift and naively swung into the passenger seat.

A short time later, Granny, surprised she hadn't come in for her hot chocolate, took a tray up to Bernice's room. She found her lying shivering on the bed, damp hair clinging to her pale face, silent sobs retching through her, the medal ribbon in shreds as Bernice frantically tore at it ripping soft skin from her fingers in the process.

"What in the name?" Granny peeled the sodden coat from her young frame. Bernice's eyes lost their sparkle and she her childhood.

Bernice thought of a dish to leave McIntosh with a bittersweet aftertaste, if all went according to plan. She wouldn't even waste a spell on him.

Maggie phoned back and relieved to hear Bernice's voicemail, left a cheery message.

'Sorry, couldn't make out what you were saying. Ears full of foam. Come round when you are ready. We can have a quick drink before we go.'

* * *

Maggie's taxi was booked for eight o'clock. She was rushing around in her undies when Bernice arrived at her door.

'Get the door would you, Stacey.'

Stacey grunted from her corner of the sofa. 'Door's open, Bernice!' she called, without getting up.

Bernice tried the handle and stepped inside the hallway. Maggie rushed past her.

'Stacey! Wish you wouldn't leave the door open. Anybody could sneak in.'

'Aye, Mammy, and they would sneak right back oot again if they clocked you in that state.'

Maggie ignored her daughter's comments and continued to run between rooms like a demented chicken.

'Earrings! Earrings!'

'Try your ears,' Bernice laughed, noticing Maggie's two gold studs were in place.

At least half a dozen discarded outfits lay strewn across the bed like deflated egos and three hairstyles aborted, before Maggie could settle on the image she wanted to portray.

'She is stressing me oot.' Stacey cradled a bottle of pink alcopops.

'Really rips my knitting too, but still, it's her big exit. Let her have her fifteen minutes.'

'She's been at it for hours, Bernice, never mind fifteen minutes.'

Bernice couldn't be bothered explaining the fifteen-minute fame thing.

'One in there for your auld auntie?'

Stacey nodded.

'Well, shift your carcass then.'

Stacey went to get a drink from the fridge, as Bernice rifled through a stack of CDs.

'I'm checking your stash for Rod Stewart.' She laughed as Stacey handed her a bottle.

'No glass?'

'Naw. Nae Rod Stewart either, Bernice. Please. Ma heid's thumpin already at the thought of this daft shindig.'

'Now…don't you go and ruin it. Stay a while, and then get into town to meet your pals. You know what your mum's like. A few sherbets and she folds like a pack of cards. I'll make sure she gets up the road.'

Maggie swaggered into the room and twirled around in front of them. The dress a safe black number.

'Catalogue. Like it?'

They both nodded, hoping to look convincing.

'Stunning.' Bernice offered her bottle. 'You sit down, I'll get another.'

'Cheers!' The three of them clinked bottles and their evening began. Bernice pretended to sip from hers.

Chapter 32

McIntosh was already in the salon when the taxi drew up. Bernice tugged at her bra to ensure her bronze-dusted cleavage was on display. The silver chain at her neck glistened, the pentagram nestling on her breasts, a talisman to keep her safe. McIntosh glanced out of the shop window, absent-mindedly throwing comments to arriving guests, inviting them to partake of the free booze set up on the counter, delighted his arson plans were snuffed by the generous offer from the council to demolish the salon to make way for sheltered housing. The salon would be razed to the ground before spring and he could walk away with a clear conscience.

Boxes of supermarket wine sat alongside a crate of bottled cider. A throng of loyal customers flowed through the doors. Scooping up peanuts and crisps and scratching at sandwich platters, they circled the venue seeking out somewhere other than treatment beds to rest.

Gulping warm Liebfraumilch from plastic beakers, the guests chattered incessantly, some reading flyers for McIntosh's latest venture, others focusing on the emptying wine boxes.

'Looking goooooooood, girl.' McIntosh offered his hand as Bernice stepped from the cab. She deliberately took her time, hoisting a long flimsy skirt subtly high enough for him to catch a glimpse of tanned flesh. A thin diamante bracelet graced her ankle, complementing metallic sandals. Bernice lingered teasingly before stepping firmly onto the pavement and letting the soft material fall gracefully to her toes. Maggie was shifting from foot to foot craning her neck to see who was in the salon, half hoping Wredd would turn up and half hoping he wouldn't in case he caused a scene.

'Here she is! Party girl!' McIntosh slurped a kiss to the side of Maggie's bobbing head as she checked the crowd of familiar faces. She wandered over to a group of squealing females at the back of the shop whilst Stacey went in search of drinks.

'Looking good, Bernice,' McIntosh drooled.

'You said.'

'How are things?'

'Doing great, thanks,' she replied through gritted teeth.

He slipped a cold finger under her pendant.

'Still into the old witchy stuff, eh?'

'You know me too well.' Bernice tilted her head. 'Like to be mysterious.'

'Is it true about the naked dancing on the beach?' He moved closer.

'Sure, and the sex with horses. All true.'

McIntosh cupped his manhood.

'Some say I'm hung like a horse.' He swiftly released the bulge and stroked Bernice's hair away from her face.

'Back soon. Someone I really want to speak to over there.' Bernice broke away.

'Jeez! The donkey,' Bernice spluttered to Stacey.

'Jesus was a donkey?' Stacey giggled.

'I was so tempted to break his hand from its spindly arm.'

'McIntosh?'

'McIntosh. Trying to entice me with his king prawn.'

'Go wind him up, it'll be fun.' Stacey swayed to the music blasting from the salon radio.

Bernice downed her wine in one and returned to McIntosh. She leaned across his shoulder. A whiff of spicy aftershave insulted her nostrils as she whispered, 'Later... Let's party.'

Leaving him with his lurid thoughts she helped herself to a soft drink and went to find Maggie.

The night progressed well. Stacey escaped around 11pm. The majority of guests left shortly after. A few stragglers and diehards mingled until after midnight, debating the worries of the world.

'Best get Maggie up the road,' Bernice told McIntosh.

He wiped a beer moustache from his saggy lips and breathed down her cleavage. 'How about coming to the casino with me?' he slurred.

Bernice, knowing he only wanted the complimentary coffee and sandwiches offered at the Chevalier, restrained herself from kicking him in the groin.

'Why don't I come back to yours? We can drop Maggie off first?' She tilted his chin upwards, directing her sexiest gaze into his pickled onion eyes.

McIntosh quickly herded the protesting revellers onto the street, anxiously shoving the leftover booze into their hands. Bernice was surprised he could move so fast.

'I knew there was always a spark there, Bernice.' He winked. 'No hard feelings...about the job I mean?'

They saw Maggie home before doubling back into town towards McIntosh's city flat. McIntosh drove slowly, with his arm resting on the open window of his prized car, a soppy melody on the radio drawing the desired attention from passers-by.

Bernice managed to restrain him up to a point on the journey and wanted the whole thing over with as quickly as possible. Judging by the blur of his eyes it wouldn't take long.

Once inside his flat she noted the garish décor, slightly perturbed by the taxidermist dream collection of stuffed animals taking up one wall of the large lounge. There was the tax word again, sneaking into her mind. He opened the balcony doors,

'You choose some music. I'll get us a drink.' He loosened his tie. 'Make yourself at home. Although I don't suppose your place is much like this?'

Bernice ignored the sarcasm and looked down onto the city below. A kaleidoscope of blurry lights mish-mashed, dancing on the surface of the river Clyde. Traffic snaked across Bells Bridge reminding her of Granny's rosary that glowed in the dark. A gift from Lourdes that somehow cheapened the sentiment. The luminous beads a stark reminder of how commercialism reaches the strangest corners of our world.

'Ever seen a water bed?' McIntosh called from another room.

Bernice despaired at this sixties throwback, convinced the offer of a martini would cause her interested façade to crumble.

'Sounds good. You got our drinks yet?' She ambled towards the stereo and slid the nearest CD into action.

Barry White tried to seduce her with dulcet tones, but only succeeded in making her giggle quietly.

'What you smiling about?' McIntosh handed her a tall-stemmed glass. Taking a sip from his own he beckoned her to join him on the low leather sofa. As she perched on the edge she felt his arm slide behind her, his fingers made her shiver.

'Like this?' He mistook her reaction for a positive one, as he fumbled to unhook her bra. Talk about going in for the kill.

'I'm a nature girl. What do you say we slip out of these clothes? I'll pop into the bathroom. Take the drinks out to the balcony, we can make love under the stars.' Bernice kissed his hand and left the room

McIntosh grunted like a bull on a promise and was soon lying in the hammock on the balcony with a cushion keeping his tackle warm. It was a cool night.

Bernice tiptoed across the floor and swiftly pulled the balcony door to a close.

She dropped the key down her cleavage and headed for the elevator.

The man hovered in the reception area, hidden behind a pillar. His initial anger diffused by the short time Bernice spent in the penthouse. He noticed the smile on her face as she left the building. Maybe it was business, all some business about the salon. Yes, that explained it. Time was running out for him now. The man wanted it over with, and soon. He watched Bernice hail a taxi. He watched the taxi drive away, blew on his hands and headed in the opposite direction.

Chapter 33

Maggie dumped her shopping on the pub floor.

'How's things?' Nick asked as he poured her a large glass of wine.

'Been better. Been worse. Wredd said anything about coming home?'

'I leave him it to it. To be fair he only really crashes here. Don't see much of him.'

'Well, I'm not giving in. If he asks you can tell him I'm actually enjoying the peace.'

'Tell him yourself. I'm no Ophray Winfrey.'

Effie leaned on the bar. 'If you ask me he's up to no good.'

'Ah yes, but nobody asked you.' Nick went to serve another customer.

Effie cleared her throat.

'Take this. I need a coffee.' Maggie slid the wine glass over to Effie.

'Thanks, hen. No sure Nick would like me drinking at the bar, but what he doesn't know won't hurt him right?' Effie took a quick gulp.

'What do you mean about Wredd?'

'I know he's your man but I've aye thought he was a bit shifty.'

'Another woman?' Maggie wasn't sure she wanted her question answered.

'Naw, mares like the horses or dodgy fags that sorta thing. Although,' Effie paused, 'I have seen him in the company of other women, but I'm sure he's just a big flirt.'

Maggie looked over at Nick. 'He's always been a gambler, Effie, but he wouldn't cheat on me. More's the pity.'

'I know what you mean, hen, give you the excuse?'

'Here, take this round the back.' She handed Effie the glass of wine. 'Enjoy.'

Maggie glanced in the mirror behind the bar.

'Refill?' the barman offered.

Maggie noticed the tattoo just below his shirt sleeve. 'Oh, hi, sorry, yeh, cappuccino. Large.'

Liam looked around for her glass.

'Oh, Effie tidied it away.' Maggie smiled. 'What's the tattoo?'

Liam pulled his sleeve up, 'Always have hope.' The words curled around a red love-heart. He quickly fastened it down again. 'Sort of family motto.'

'Loving your accent.'

'Thanks.'

'My best friend's from up north.'

'Is he?'

'She.'

'You need to stay out back.' Nick took over and waited until Liam went back to the kitchen. 'Nice lad but I told him, no bar work until he proves himself with the donkey work.'

'Youngsters these days eh, Nick? You getting too old for the donkey work yourself?'

'Nope. I think it does 'em good to work the cellars and stuff before draping across the bar chatting up the customers.'

'Sure, Nick. Cos that's your job right?' Maggie slammed a ten-pound note on the bar and took up a seat at a nearby table. She sat with her back to the bar and finished her drink.

The bar was getting busy. Nick took the note back to Maggie.

'On the house.' He laid ten pounds on the table. 'Is this mood because Wredd was a no show at your leaving do?'

Maggie scowled at him. 'Wredd, Bernice…everything.'

'Let me join you.' Nick swiftly placed a paper napkin in front of her. 'A few dark shadows under your eyes there. I'll grab a coffee.'

'Pots calling kettles black,' she replied. 'Anyway the bar's filling up, you'd better go.'

'You what?' Nick was busy frothing milk at the cappuccino

machine.

'Oh, nothing.' Maggie skimmed a layer of froth with her tongue and cradled the mug in her hands, staring thoughtfully at the bubbles.

'You okay?' Nick sat across from her, forcing Maggie meet his gaze. 'Bernice is a free spirit, Maggie.'

'Nothing in this life is free.'

'Leave her to sort herself out and she will.'

'You sound like Wredd.' She stirred her coffee. 'Where is he anyway?'

'Haven't seen him for a while, thought you two might have kissed and made up by now?'

'You think?' Maggie stirred her coffee again. 'He been asking about me, at all?'

Nick shook his head. 'Wredd doesn't appreciate you.' Nick changed the subject. 'But Bernice relies on you, stubborn as she is, she needs your friendship.'

'How do you know what she needs? A few drunken fumbles and you think that's all there is to her?' Maggie strummed her fingers on the bar. 'Maybe she's right, all men are bastards.'

Nick topped up her coffee. 'I work long hours in here. Complicated relationships are the last thing on my mind. You could be looking at the next Peter Stringfellow!'

'Peter Pan more likes. You're as bad as Bernice. What age are you now, Nick? Thirty-seven, thirty-eight? Still chasing rainbows.'

'Getting the conservatory extended this year. Room for a dance floor. Maybe I'll call it the Rainbow Room?'

Maggie managed a wry smile. 'Good for you.'

He clasped his hands around hers and lowered the coffee mug. 'Tell Uncle Nick all about it.'

The tears fell freely as Maggie unburdened her worries. In a disjointed garble she explained about the letters Bernice was determined to follow up, and the gambling debts Wredd left her with.

Effie was at the bar, polishing beer pumps.

'Take the wheel would you!' Nick called to her.

Effie dropped the duster and turned to exclaim her dissatisfaction at being his dogsbody. She caught sight of Maggie, crumpled over an empty cup, an avalanche of soggy tissues surrounding her like fallen lilies.

Effie decided to keep quiet.

'I'll bring us a couple of soda waters,' Nick said. 'Come on through, Wredd's probably on a bender somewhere.' Nick ushered Maggie towards the back room. She never gave any thought to where he lived, assuming his flat was somewhere close, but not actually on the premises. Nick always seemed to be propping up the bar exchanging gossip and advice with his customers.

'How come you don't drink? Isn't it a bit odd for a pub landlord?'

'Not when your old man pickled himself every night and literally peed your inheritance against the wall.'

'Oh, I'd forgotten about your dad's place. It was a cracking wee inn. Function suite and everything. What happened then?'

'Oh, same old, same old. He never went to sleep at night, more like lost consciousness. My mother got fed up and legged it with a rep from the brewery. Left us to it. I was only fifteen at the time.'

'I know about your mother, remember? You've never seen her since?'

'Nope. Last I heard she was set up in a bar in the Costa Brava.'

'And now you're here.'

'Not much, but it's home and I know the ropes.' Nick slid a few car magazines to the floor, indicating that Maggie could sit on the huge black leather pouffe taking up most of the floorspace. She slumped onto the cold fabric.

'Not used to having visitors.' Nick kicked a pair of scuffed shoes under the television set.

'You live here? In the bar?' Maggie was momentarily distracted by the discovery.

'Sure do. Saves a second mortgage. I don't need a lot of space.'

Maggie looked at Nick. His hair was already thinning, although he'd attempted to spike it up with gel. Laughter lines bordered his eyes. He gently laid his arm around her shoulders.

'Oh where did it all go wrong, Nick?' Maggie trembled.

'Poor choices, but then we move on. Bernice needs to go her own way too and you need to make Wredd pay his share, even if you don't take him back.'

Maggie sat quietly tearing at a box of tissues.

'Maggie. Do you ever wonder what would have happened if I hadn't gone away?'

'We were teenagers, Nick.'

'You didn't have to marry so young.'

'Really?'

'You know I was well and truly hurt when I came back. You and Wredd? I never saw that coming.'

'How could you see anything from the distance you put between us? Five months you were gone and not a word.'

'I was in a bad place, what with mum leaving.'

'Oh and I was in Disneyland.'

'Why do you put up with him, Maggie?'

'He's been a good dad to Stacey.'

'And that's enough for you?'

'He stood by me.'

Nick shifted in his chair. 'I still love you,' he whispered.

Maggie stared ahead. 'Sorry, Nick. Sorry. I was miles away. Look I'd better go. I've taken up enough of your time.'

'No worries, Maggie. I'm always here.' He spread his arms wide offering a hug. 'Day and night.'

Maggie hugged him briefly and hurried towards the door. She stopped, dabbed her eyes and asked, 'Please, Nick, not a word to anyone, about Bernice, or Wredd.'

'What about them?' Nick smiled, reassuring Maggie her secrets were safe. If she stayed a bit longer, he might have shared a secret of his own. Kicking the door closed he leaned his forehead against it. The spark of a flame could be rekindled or permanently snuffed out. Nick knew the flame in his mind could flourish, if only Maggie would give it a chance.

He looked around the small room; sparse, odds and ends of other people's discarded furniture, practical. Wredd's stuff was still taking up space. As he shoved it to one side, a pile of betting slips fell from a shoe box.

He thought of his own mother and wondered if she would ever coming looking for him. Bernice never got the chance to know her son, Nick's mother never wanted to.

'Nick! I really need a hand through here!' Effie's frazzled voice rose above a loud thud on the door.

'Be right there!' Nick called back, wiping sticky hands on denim-clad thighs. He glanced briefly around the room and checked his face in the mirror.

'Everything okay?' Effie asked as Nick returned to the bar.

'Fine, Effie, just keeping the customers sweet.'

Nick spent most of his days in the bar, or at the brewery negotiating discounts. Friday mornings he could be found at the farmers market bartering for the weekend specials. The occasional fling with Desiree at the bakers, ensured batches of baguettes and croissants arrived daily, with invoices rarely following. Jean at the fish stall was another conquest, supplying gourmet lobster at haddock prices. Nick convinced himself that providing all were happy, then he was not doing anything wrong. Still, occasionally he felt alone, even in the crowded bar.

Once the rush was over Nick perched on the edge of a bar stool running fingers through his sticky locks in concentration.

'You two look good together.' Effie sat beside him and shot soda into a tumbler half filled with ice.

'Maggie? Come on Effie we've never been anything more than friends. Anyway,' he ruffled her hair, 'you know you're the only woman in my life.'

'Nick! Your hands are all tacky.' She backed away from him laughing and headed for the kitchen.

Nick thought of Bernice, her mood swings. He envied her exuberance for life, loved the way her laughter rang out in melodic bursts. He knew now all her actions were a camouflage. Now he understood. How did he miss the charade? Could he have helped? Nick justified their rendezvous as being all Bernice wanted. Why did he never ask her? He often woke from an encounter troubled by mixed feelings – joy at having shared such intimacy with Bernice, and relief that was as far as it would ever go.

'I don't need a woman in my life,' he mumbled, 'especially one with emotional baggage.'

Chapter 34

Maggie was shocked when Bernice turned up the next afternoon and relayed her story about McIntosh, but she soon softened.

'As long as he doesn't report you for assault.'

'As if. And admit moi, a mere slip of a female, got the best of him. He deserved much worse.'

Bernice and Maggie were enjoying a coffee in Maggie's living room.

'Stacey won't speak to me, but I'm sure something is wrong.' Maggie carved a chunk of Madeira cake and slipped it onto a tea plate.

'Says she's taking a study break. They do take breaks don't they? Students.'

'She's seeing someone. Someone here, in Glasgow.'

'So! Maggie, you were worried about her getting too serious with that Jasper character. Surely it's better if she shops around?'

'Jason. But she hasn't told me she's stopped seeing Jason. Not sure if she's two-timing him or what?'

'What what what Watson?' Bernice helped herself to the last piece of cake. 'Shes playing the field. If she were a boy you wouldn't think anything of it would you?

Maggie scooped crumbs from the table into her hand. 'You've never been one for high morals, Bernice. Don't know why I'm confiding in you.'

'Because I'm your friend, Maggie. Your true friend. And hey! My morals are totally fine.'

'Wredd says I only have you as a friend because I'm too scared to have you as an enemy.'

'Wredd talks through a gap in his buttocks.'

'I know, but really I'm more worried about Stacey. It's like maybe Jason dumped her? Maybe she is going for this new guy on the rebound? Maybe she's going off with lots of boys?'

'And maybe you should remember what you were up to at her age?'

'I was naïve. It's different now girls have more choice, higher aspirations.'

'You got pregnant at eighteen, so marriage came along quicker than you'd have liked, but at least the big dud made an honest woman of you.'

'He didn't. Wredd didn't make an honest woman of me.' Maggie topped up her coffee.

'So you didn't marry? You two been living over the broom all this time?

'No. We married. Wredd worked away a lot, oil rigs; he wasn't here when Stacey was born.'

'So? Lots of fathers miss the birth. I know those two argue hammer and tongs but he's like argumentative with everyone.'

'It's more important. Wredd didn't only miss the birth, he missed the conception.'

Bernice choked and spluttered cake crumbs over her top.

'I hate him, Bernice, he makes my skin crawl.'

'I'll help, Maggie. What are friends for? I've got some things with me.'

As they set up the altar and stones Maggie became morbidly excited. Bernice explained the Wiccan way was not to cause harm.

'So there is to be no Action Man doll getting battered to bits by these stones?'

'No, Maggie, rise above the anger.'

Bernice unravelled a silk cloth and placed a small photo of Wredd onto the centre. She dripped clear honey onto the photo before wrapping the cloth around it very slowly until she created the shape of a five-pointed star. Maggie recognised the pentagram symbol.

'I bind thee. I bind thee. I bind thee!' Bernice tied fine silver thread around the silk parcel. 'Now put this in the freezer.'

'What?'

'He is bound in golden sweet light, he cannot bring you harm, frozen in time.'

'So no Action Man? Pins? Scorching flames?'

'Back of the freezer, best place for him.'

Maggie had never felt such pleasure since she found her first pair of high-heels in the back of the shed the previous summer.

Bernice was on a roll and continued to whisper, 'The ice is a reflection of your own feelings, how you feel cold towards him. Leave it in there for twenty-eight days. From midnight tonight leave the crystals on your altar, light the white candle and mourn the death of your relationship in silence. On the twenty-ninth day take the parcel from the freezer and lay it outdoors in the heart of the bluebell woods. Offer it to the Goddess. Release him to find his own true love. The sun will melt the ice restoring warmth and love to your heart. Mother Nature will gently discard your offering over time, and as she does so, your heart will heal.'

Bernice ended the session with a final reading of the Tarot.

'Now you have the strength to let him go, you don't need Wredd in your life.'

Maggie smiled.

'Who is Stacey's…'

They heard a crash outside the front window.

Maggie pulled back the curtains to be faced with Wredd lying sprawled across the gravel path. Wredd waved up at her and smiled, stumbling to get to his feet. He only made it to his knees, hovering on all fours.

Bernice looked over Maggie's shoulder, laughing. Maggie shrugged her off and barged past her into the garden. Wredd's knees were grazed and poking through his jeans. He was clutching a tree.

'Is he carrying a tree?' Bernice joined Maggie outside.

'For you, my darling wife, for you to hug.' He gestured his

free arm towards Maggie.

'It is a tree!' Bernice was almost hysterical with laughter.

'Shut up and help me get him inside.' Maggie pulled at Wredd and dumped him inside the hallway. They helped him stand. He swayed down towards the tree laid on the path, its roots firmly planted in a large ceramic pot.

'It's a wishing tree,' Wredd cackled, 'ravaged from Mother Earth, and rescued by your truly.' He hiccupped loudly.

'Help me get him inside, Bernice.'

'I'm going nowhere without my tree,' Wredd slurred. 'We can all hug it together, communal cuddles. Good for the soul.'

Maggie shoved him into the hallway. 'Bernice will get the tree.' Turning to her friend she hissed, 'Get it in, before someone sees it.'

Bernice struggled to lift the tree, so instead dragged it over the steps and into the front porch. She locked the door and stood the pot upright. It was a nice tree. With a sturdy stem and bulbous green foliage cut like a Christmas bauble. The pot rim was chipped. Bernice dragged it further into the hall, still laughing. She could hear Maggie arguing with Wredd in the front room.

'Jist nipping down to Nick's. We'll talk later, Maggie,' she shouted towards the living room door, and grabbing her jacket, headed off into the early evening.

As Wredd lost consciousness on the sofa, Maggie removed his shoes and placed them beside the TV. She didn't attempt to get his jacket off. Despite her anger, Maggie went through the all-too-familiar routine, plucking a quilt from the airing cupboard. She filled a glass with cold water and left it on the table beside the sofa. Wredd grunted. Maggie decided the kitchen basin might save a load of cleaning in the morning. She laid it on the floor beside her snoring lump of a husband.

Maggie headed back to the kitchen to look for a strong drink. She found plenty to choose from and settled on a large brandy. It stung her throat and burned her stomach, but was just what she needed.

Grasping the bottle by the neck she flicked off the kitchen light and headed to her room. She reached for the photo beside her bed, glanced at the happy trio in the broken frame, and turned it face down.

Resting back on the pillows, she closed her eyes. She thought of how she would tackle Wredd the next day as she pressed speed dial on the phone beside her bed.

'Nick? Hi it's me, Maggie. Look, Wredd is off the rails again, I could do with some help.'

Nick was busy in the bar. 'Bad timing, Maggie. It's jumping in here. We'll talk through the week, okay?'

Maggie listened to the burr of the line, and slapped the phone down in despair.

Chapter 36

The next morning arrived all too soon.

The bedroom was bright. Far too bright for Maggie's headache. She shielded her eyes and checked the clock. For a moment she couldn't remember what day it was. Her mouth felt dry, her breath foul. The half-empty bottle on the side cabinet reminded her why. She could barely look at it. Turning the other way, she swung her legs to the side of the bed and groped around for slippers. She rubbed her temple sensing the pain building up behind her eyeballs. She still wore her clothes. Sweaty and crumpled she took them off and instinctively wrapped her dressing gown around herself. What was she doing drinking mid-week? She smoothed the quilt roughly over the bed and lifted three decorative cushions from the floor, throwing them randomly towards the pine headboard, thinking of the bedroom makeover she wasted so much time on. On the scale of problems in her life, what did it matter?

Wredd was awake when Maggie entered the living room. He sat on the sofa, his eyes two dark smudges with hair like thick tangled rope; taking long, slow draws from a cigarette.

'I wish you wouldn't smoke in here,' Maggie commented on her way past to the kitchen.

Wredd cupped the cigarette in his hand and tried to wave the smoke away. He looked around for an ashtray.

'No ashtrays, Maggie?'

'No smoking, Wredd. Take it outside.'

The cigarette squashed a burnt hole across the midriff of some B-list celebrity on the cover of a magazine.

'I'll get the tea, Maggie,' he offered. Maggie was already banging dishes around in the kitchen and ignored him, each thump echoing in Wredd's head.

'I said I'll get the tea,' Wredd repeated louder, pulling the quilt away from where it was tangled around his legs. He stood and folded it neatly, plumped up the two pillows and lifted the empty basin.

Maggie returned and sat on the big armchair opposite him, clutching a mug of tea. Wredd stood with the basin in his hand.

'Where's mine?'

'You don't live here anymore,' Maggie said loudly, taking a sip.

Wredd sighed and scratched his head. He sat down, holding the basin on his knee. 'Come on, Maggie, I won a stash. It was a wild night.'

'I don't care.' Maggie's voice was calm and determined. 'I'm done, Wredd. I can't take any more. You were right to move out.'

'Look, I know I was a bit over the top.' Wredd looked down at his feet. 'I can't actually remember what happened last night, but since I ended up on the couch with the hangover kit, I take it you are less than pleased?'

Maggie didn't reply. Wredd stared at her.

Maggie slammed her mug down and stormed out of the room.

Stacey passed her in the hallway and slouched down beside Wredd, hooking her arm into his. She rested her head on Wredd's shoulder.

'She is pretty pissed off,' Stacey offered. 'But it was funny.'

'I can't remember the details, but I must have been well out of order for your mum to throw a strop like this.'

Their conversation was interrupted by the phone ringing.

Stacey leaned over and answered it. She listened for a few seconds, held her hand over the mouthpiece, and looked at Wredd. 'It's for you.'

Wredd scratched his eyebrows and pointed to his chest. He laid the phone against his ear. 'Erh, hello.'

The voice coming through was coarse and loud. 'You've got twenty-four hours tae bring ma tree back!' The line went dead.

Wredd turned to Stacey who was clutching her knees to her chin and rolling from side to side on the couch.

'What the...?' Wredd's mouth formed a huge O. His eyes blinked quickly.

'The tree, Dad.'

'Tree?'

Stacey ran to the door and pulled it ajar. The tree stood innocently in the pot in the hallway.

'It is a tree,' Wredd acknowledged, 'but from where and who wants it back?'

'You tell me. You're the one who brought it home.'

Maggie came back into the room fully clothed, and scooped up the folded bedding.

'I'll get the blankets,' Wredd offered.

Maggie turned her back on him. The next thing Wredd and Stacey heard was the front door slamming.

'I've done it this time.' Wredd followed Stacey back into the kitchen and watched as she put bread in the toaster. 'What am I going to do?'

Here he was, a grown man, asking the advice of his daughter.

Stacey took a chunk of cheese from the fridge, sniffed it, and checked the sell-by date on the label.

'Dunno, Dad. Maybe she'll calm doon later.'

Stacey and Wredd started to plough through a rack of toast.

'Don't suppose you know where I got the tree?' Wredd asked. 'He sounded really threatening on the phone.'

'Aye. I do. It wiz frae ootside the bar. Nick saw you take it but let it go. He knows you'll take it back. Probably one of the punters having a laugh.'

'When did they get trees?'

'Och it wiz fur Jinty McFadden's wedding reception. One for each side oh the door, but someone beat you to it earlier in the night, or you could have got a pair.' Stacey ripped a corner off the bread and dipped it into her mug.

'You are disgusting!' Wredd pushed the plate away. 'Will you help me take it back?'

'Suppose so,' Stacey agreed. 'After I catch a snooze.'

Wredd noticed Bernice's hat hanging on the radiator.

'Bernice here last night again?'

Stacey was already upstairs. Wredd punched the worktop.

He dialled the phone number the van driver gave him earlier. This time it rang. He listened eagerly and smiled at the enthusiasm of the voice on the line. Mrs McEwan was delighted at the unexpected call.

"Yes, very interesting.' Wredd scribbled some notes down. 'Oh, I understand, I'll be discreet. Yes, I appreciate it, of course you only want to help.'

Wredd couldn't believe how easy it was to prompt the responses, and when he heard them couldn't believe how bizarre they sounded.

'Really ill was she? Oh I'm sure she would want all of her family together. Yes.'

'And you say the boy's here now? In Glasgow?'

Wredd laughed. 'No, no, you've been more than helpful. Of course, of course, soul of discretion.'

'Beauty!'

He punched the air and grinned. "Best wear my lucky pants today. A quick snifter and off to the dogs."

* * *

Wredd stopped off at the benefits centre. 'Hiya, Carol, how good do you look?'

The pretty receptionist patted her hair and leaned across the counter. 'Come to sign on? Surely not?'

'Come to see my favourite spy.'

'Spy?'

'Sure, like a James Bond girl. You've got the looks.'

The girl blushed and sucked the end of her pen. 'Really, Wredd, what are you after?'

'Outside?'

The girl looked across at a colleague. 'Cover me for five?'

In the forecourt the girl leant back. Wredd pressed his hands on the wall above her shoulders. 'Say a kid was to come here for the summer, looking for work like, what would his first stop be?'

'Here probably. At the jobcentre.'

Wredd tilted her chin upwards. 'Beauty and brains. I'm looking for someone.'

'You forgotten that you're married?' the girl teased.

'I'm looking for a young bloke, from the islands. Turned up in the last few weeks.'

'Variety really must be the spice.'

'Doing a favour for a friend. Anyway, you could check up new registrations?'

'Seriously? Ever heard of the Official Secrets Act?'

'I can keep a secret.' Wredd leaned in and kissed her forehead. 'Not sure where in the city.'

'Name, date of birth? NI number? Occupation?'

'Erh, probably, about nineteen – twenty years old, maybe a year either way,' Wredd paused, 'and probably ginger. I don't have anything else.'

'Nutter. Meet me at Nick's, in an hour?'

Wredd headed for the bookmakers feeling his luck was changing.

* * *

Carol walked into the bar carrying a large brown envelope. Wredd stood to greet her. 'Sure, I'll never breathe a word.' He tried to grab the envelope from Carol's hand.

'Nothing illegal?'

'Course it's nothing dodgy. Doing a friend a favour. Re-uniting family, like Cilla Black.'

'Her with the teeth,' Carol giggled.

'Teeth and red hair.'

'Child-Line?'

'Not Esther Rantzen daftie. Cilla Black. Red hair.'

'I'd have loved having red hair. Exotic so it is. Sexy. Like Bernice.'

'Go grab a seat. I'll get you a drink.' Wredd took the envelope and stuffed it inside his coat.

Carol sauntered across the half-empty bar. A young couple sat nearby holding hands.

Carol sat at the next table and leaned across to speak to them.

'You think red hair is sexy?' Carol asked.

'Oh go for strawberry blonde,' the girl replied.

Wredd placed a bottle of wine beside Carol. 'Excuse me, going to see a man about a dog.'

The chill of the ice bucket was still on his hands as he left.

The man sat in one of the booths in Nick's bar with a newspaper in front of him. He circled sections slowly, studying the text. He glanced at the big clock above the bar and checked his watch. It was going to plan, everything in place. He only needed to choose the right moment.

Chapter 37

Dermott sat in Thomas's flat in the west end of Oban.

'Haven't seen Liam for days.'

Dermott scratched his head.

'Where else would he go?'

'Sure, I know there was one kick off too many with the old man, but I never thought he'd go through with it like.'

'Through with what?' Dermott perched on the edge of the sofa.

'Liam said he promised yir ma he'd find something. Something she lost a while back.'

'Something? Or someone?'

'He said it was family business, never went into detail.' Thomas picked at his fingernails.

'Tell me what you know.'

Thomas anxiously ripped at his cuticles till they bled.

'He said something about Glasgow.'

'If he does show up. Tell him to come home. No one's angry. We need to talk.' Dermott lifted his holdall. 'I'm away to make a call.'

Dermott rummaged for loose change at the nearest phone booth.

'Robbie? How's the old man?' Dermott clutched his middle and remembered he'd skipped breakfast. 'Good. Good. I've told you, keep him topped up. I'll check in later or sooner if I have any news.'

'I don't like this, Dermott. Sure you know he'll go off on one if he knows you've gone after him.'

'There's stuff you don't know, Robbie. Stuff I never knew.'

'So? Leave it be. If the old man never told us he doesn't wants us poking our neb in now.'

'I'm with Thomas on the mainland. You keep your head down

and say nothing.'

'Is Liam there too?'

Dermott paused. 'There go the beeps, I'll call later.'

Chapter 38

Tonsillitis brought Bernice to her knees. The cruel morning sun tore at her face, scratching her awake. Her back ached as her tongue lolled heavy with dehydration. She turned onto her belly and snuggled beneath the duvet dropping effortlessly back to sleep.

The rattle of keys on the worktop disturbed Bernice's slumber.

'Is it you, Maggie?' she croaked.

'No. It's a burglar'

Bernice patted her head to make sure it was still attached and swung her legs up to a wobbly stance. Slipping her French-manicured toes into soft beaded mules she inhaled sharply.

'Bad night?' Maggie asked.

'Bad timing.' Bernice's face was flushed, as she coughed drily.

The chime of the front door bell diverted their attention.

'Probably him. Wredd looking for you,' Bernice snorted. 'Tell him to go to hell!'

Maggie stormed off, flip-flopping across the tiled hallway.

'Tell slut features I don't do threesomes. You can have monkey man all to yourself.' Bernice held a bag of ice to her forehead.

The doorbell rang. Rang and rang again.

'Give us a minute!' Maggie muttered under her breath, pulling open the door.

The man appeared startled by the unfriendly welcome. He pressed his hand against the stained glass of the door and wedged his foot on the plinth.

'Do you mind?' Maggie shrieked.

'I do actually.' He peered into the hallway. 'I need to see Bernadette O'Hanlon?'

Glancing over her shoulder into the hallway, the man caught a glimpse of a body slumped on a battered chaise longue.

'Please,' he whispered, as the figure came into focus; copper curls gleaming against the green velvet of her robe. 'Is she okay? What's going on?'

Maggie shuffled to avoid his gaze. 'There is no Bernadette here,' she lied. Pulling the door towards the stairway Maggie hissed. 'If you're here about the letters you can sling your hook. We've already told the police.'

'I don't know about any letters? I need to speak to Bernadette. Please?'

'It's a wee sin fur me so it is!" came a garbled voice from along the hallway.

Hands on hips Maggie coughed loudly. 'Wait a minute.' She called back, 'Bernice, you expecting visitors?'

Leaving the door chain on, she tottered over to the jumble of limbs and tapped Bernice's shoulder. Bernice tried to focus momentarily then blanked out with a loud snort. Maggie returned to the unexpected guest who stayed silent, but deter-mined. 'Now is really not a good time.' Forcing a smile she tried to think of something bright to say. 'Look I know who you are; Bernice is not very well, she's not up for visitors. I suggest you leave before you do any more harm.'

The man reluctantly scribbled some numbers on the back of a used ferry ticket. 'I really need to see her, to sort things out. I'm only here a few more days at most.'

'If you know anything about her son, why not tell her?' Maggie spat. 'She's given you all she has and more. You're breaking a good woman's heart!' she called as he backed down the stairs.

Maggie tucked Bernice under the duvet and tiptoed from the flat.

Bernice was once again reminiscing in her dreams.

"But, Granny, it's still light. Please can I stay out and play?"

Granny smiled as she ruffled Bernice's hair.

"What am I going to do with you?" she laughed. 'Bath time. Then bedtime. Granddad will be home soon and you know he likes to enjoy his tea in peace."

Minutes later Bernice was in front of the coal fire being sanded down by the remains of a bath towel. Shivering as she struggled into the nightie Granny held for her.

"Please tell me a story, Granny."

The smell of carbolic soap, even the scraping of the bone comb over her scalp, felt comforting. Warmth enveloped her thin body as Bernice sat on Granny's knee and listened to her adventures. With the crocheted rug wrapped tightly around them both it was easy to transport herself to Granny's world of magic and make believe.

Recognising the heavy footsteps crunch the gravel outside, Granny's mood quickly changed. She snuffed out the candles, packing them quickly into the bottom of the dresser, opening the window to quell the waft of incense.

"Quick! Quick! It's your granddad. Off to bed now." Granny's expression softened as she landed a kiss on Bernice's forehead. "Ssssh not a sound."

Bernice caught a glimpse of Granddad's shadow through the frosted glass panels on the big double doors. She scurried off to tumble into the double bed she shared with Robbie and Dermott. They were not family although Granddad always called them his "boys". Tam McShane gave no time to his sons. Not since his wife left them all when she could stand his beatings no longer. It suited Granddad to give them food and board in return for working on the farm.

Bernice jammed herself between the snoring boys, embedded in the warm cocoon, knowing she would be disturbed when one or the other of them failed to wake in time to use the pot under the bed. Come morning, Granddad would be angry and she would take the blame.

Saturdays were different. Granny polished Granddad's boots on a Saturday and laid them outside the parlour door, like a trophy of her dedication to her marriage. The boots were huge. One day Bernice tried them on but they gobbled up her feet and she couldn't walk with them.

Granddad caught her, and taking off his belt swiped her across the head with it.

"Bloody eejit," he roared.

Granny dressed the children in their best clothes on a Saturday, ready to visit Mrs McEwan, a neighbour, up the road. Mrs McEwan was the local postmistress and all-round gossipmonger, but Granny, like the other women in the village, considered her a confidant.

Lined up in the kitchen like soldiers on parade ready for inspection, the two boys would soon get bored and chase each other around until Granny became nervous and putting her fingers to her lips she'd whisper, "Sssssh, Granddad's been working hard all week. Let him lie."

One time Granddad came bursting into the kitchen and lunged straight for Bernice. The strength of his clout knocked her sideways. She staggered across the room and falling caught her elbow on the side of the stone sink.

"Bloody eeejit. You help yer granny." Turning to the boys he yelled, "Keep that wee gob shite quiet. Can't a man get peace in his ain hoose?"

The left side of Bernice's face was numb for hours, and the pain in her elbow lasted all day, but when Granny asked, she smiled and said she was fine.

Mrs McEwan lived above the post office, set between the butchers and grocers. Bernice could read the name on the back of the buses thundering past as the troupe made their weekly trudge towards the village. The boys whinged and cried to get on the bus, but Granny always said the fresh air would do them good. So they walked the two miles there and back every weekend.

"For better for worse, best try and keep out of his way." Mrs McEwan stuffed home baking into Granny's bag as she complained about Granddad's erratic behaviour. Granddad was always waiting at the front gate when they got home.

"Is this it? Miserable auld cow."

Granny trembled as he emptied her purse. Sometimes he turned so fast Bernice didn't know which way to move. Granddad would make her choice for her as he pushed her aside, taking the back of his hand across her face.

"Bloody eejit! Get oot ma road."

"Sssssorrrry," Bernice stammered, as though it were her fault.

The last time, she never felt the blow, but heard the crack as her head hit the fence; Bernice tasted blood in her mouth. Granddad, the hero of the Pig and Bull, laughed and bolted down the path waving down a passing truck.

When the neighbours came, Granny pleaded with Bernice to tell them she tripped over her slippers. Granny looked frightened, so Bernice told them she fell even though they both knew it was a lie.

Chapter 39

Later, in the early hours, Bernice was curled in a corner inside her hallway, like an alert feline waiting to pounce. The light reflected from the stained glass windows of the front door panels, creating a mystical glow around her. A crystal prism swayed lightly in the breeze casting tiny rainbow patterns on the walls.

'Come on, come on.' She focused on the letterbox. Hours passed. Bernice felt a cramp in her leg. She stood up and stamped her numb feet hard. It was chilly in the hallway. She looked towards her open bedroom door wondering if she could quickly snatch the duvet.

With her eyes on the letterbox, Bernice reached inside the room and tugged. The quilt slid off the bed and she was soon snuggled within it.

The letters were always there early Friday mornings. No postmark. This time Bernice would be there first.

The night dragged on. When she woke, the letter was there. Forgetting her anger at missing the delivery, Bernice tore the envelope open. The content grew with each letter, as did the financial demands. Bernice read the figure twice.

Bernice looked around her flat, thinking of how happy she felt in her nest despite everything. A Tiffany lamp sat lopsided on the sideboard. Bernice leaned over and ruffled the fringed edge. A few beads slipped onto the floor. She bent to pick them up, admiring the amber tinge. She held the beads tightly in her closed fist.

'Oh, Hex. Looks like we'll have to store our lives in bubble wrap. But don't you worry, it won't be for a while yet.' Bernice walked around the small flat.

She leaned to the back of the shelf and dislodged one of the wooden panels, pulling out a thick velvet bag.

Kneeling on the floor, she pulled the bag's gold-coloured drawstring. A selection of jewellery fell onto the carpet. Bernice gently lifted a small wicker box from another shelf and set the contents down. A purple strip of velvet lay crumpled in front of her. She smoothed the soft material and set up her altar. Sitting in front of it she took a pack of tarot cards from a black silk pouch. Sprinkling white crystals onto her palm, she cleansed the cards with sea salt and spread them in front of her. One by one she noted the symbols as she spread them carefully before returning them to the darkness. She lit a blue candle and stared into the flame. Closing her eyes she whispered, 'Let me feel the silver light. Let it seep into my body, energise my thoughts and lighten my soul. Show me a sign.'

Hex rolled three small marbles towards her. They settled close to her knees. Each held a bronzed bead. As the cat playfully brushed soft paws against the glass, they reflected the candle's flame. The small heap of jewellery glistened. Bernice knew it was a temporary solution. She tidied everything back onto the shelves.

'Thanks, Hex, you are such a smart cat. Need to head into town now.'

* * *

Soon, Bernice was in the city centre, hidden by the crowds as she searched for her destination. The shop was partially obscured by an old billboard blown from its fixings in a recent storm. Set at the end of a narrow cobbled lane, it was the only window with a dull glow of light. The others were boarded with graffiti-decorated shutters. Bernice's hands were warm as she placed them against her cold cheeks, giving her face a brief slap. Three huge brass balls hung precariously above the doorway. A sign in the window read: "We buy junk. We sell antiques."

Hovering at the entrance, Bernice smirked at the traditional symbol hanging heavy overhead. *Golden balls.* She stumbled across the doorstep trying to adjust her eyes to the dimly lit interior of the Aladdin's cave. There was stuff everywhere, lumped in piles and corners, electric flex trailing from bundles of fur, huge cans of paint plonked on top of books. All sorts. A scrawny youth hung over the public side of a wooden counter, thin hands grasping at the metal screen separating him from the decrepit-looking gent on the other side.

'Och man. Ma burds up the duff. Need a cot and stuff know whit ah mean?'

The older man behind the mesh slid a heavy gold-coloured chain back towards the youth.

'I'm doing you a favour, son. It's my last offer.'

Scooping the chain up from the hollow of the counter, the younger man spat angrily at the shopkeeper. 'Robbin bastart!' He shoved it back towards him, grabbing the banknotes as they slid beneath the screen. He knocked against Bernice and hurried outside.

Bernice approached the counter cautiously and offered her wares, both parties knowing the desperation of her actions. The old man lifted various pieces and wedged an eyeglass over his left eye, and squinted at each in turn. Bernice watched his face for any sign of excitement.

'Wouldn't like to play poker with you.' She smiled nervously.

He counted out a few notes, and seeing her disappointed expression added a couple more before refolding the wad back into his pocket.

Bernice hesitated for a moment, tears welling in her eyes.

It's only trinkets, she told herself as they silently sealed the transaction.

'Mission accomplished!' Bernice declared to no one in particular as she left the shop with a heavy purse and light heart.

Chapter 40

The old man wedged his wheelchair in the doorway of the small shop. 'A tin of me usual,' he called.

Mrs McEwan was deep in conversation, but on hearing his voice she quickly wrapped the cheese she was slicing and stuffed it into her customer's basket, waving her away. 'I'll be putting it on your slate. No problem.'

'Would you shift, woman? I've better things to be doing than hanging around this here aul post office.'

'Sure, sure, Mr O'Hanlon. Golden Virginia. You okay for papers?' The tobacco was barely in his hand but he was rolling a fresh cigarette with the skill of an origami artist. Lighting up, he took a deep draw, then broke into a coughing fit.

'I was sorry to hear.'

'Save it for the Women's Guild, you aul crow.'

Robbie rushed across from the Pig and Bull. 'What you up to now? I take a visit to the lav and you go and do this.'

'Let me be!' The old man clutched the wheels of the chair and rowed back towards the pub.

'Don't be selling him any more baccy.'

'Like I'm going to say no to a good customer.' Mrs McEwan took her chance. 'Not seen Dermott?'

'He's away, not away, busy sorting things.'

'Away? Not away? Busy doing what?' Mrs McEwan moved closer. 'Rumour has it he's heading for the mainland? Left you in the lurch. Seems to be a bit of a tradition lately what with the wee fella heading off only last week.'

Robbie shifted from one foot to another picking at invisible threads on his jacket.

'You can tell me, son, I'm a friend of the family.'

'Nothing to tell. Liam's taking a break. Dermott's gone to tell him about Ma. He'll bring him home.'

'The way I heard it, the old man lost his rag with the wee fella? Asking too many questions was he?'

Robbie was already hurrying to catch up with the old man.

'Truth will come out you know. Always does.' Mrs McEwan's voice faded in the wind.

Chapter 41

Liam waited in the café, hands clutched around a bottle of coke. A couple of taxi drivers sat across the room.

'I was lucky I never got killed.' Gerry MacPhee was holding court. 'Bumps and bruises, Poor guy in the truck, shaking like a jelly he was.'

'How'd it happen then?'

'Puncture. He spun right out of control. Polish I think he was.'

'What was the polis doing driving a truck?'

'Numptie. The guy's from Krakow, brand new so he is. They stuck us in a side ward for a coupla days, got on like nobody's business.'

Liam checked his watch. The group of drivers laughed and wolfed down rolls on Lorne sausage.

'Could 'ave sued the bugga.'

'Sued him for what? It was a puncture I tell you, tyre exploded like a firework.'

'He should sue the company.'

'Cash in hand though. He told me. Clever guy as well, driving a truck.'

'So? We drive cabs.'

'Oh hello there!' Gerry called as Stacey walked into the café.

She nodded towards him and smiled. Liam pushed back his chair and pulled another one out from the table.

'You want a drink? Cake?'

'Careful, son,' Gerry called over. 'It'll be champagne and wedding cake afore you know it!'

The drivers settled their bill as Gerry playfully slapped Liam on the back. Looking at Stacey he took off his bunnet and said, 'Still, you won't need a choir, not with this one's voice.'

'You a singer?' Liam asked.

'Like an angel.' Gerry laughed as he left.

Liam passed Stacey the menu.

'Angel Delight.'

'Is it your stage name? Sounds like a stripper.'

A young waitress stood by with a notepad and pencil poised. Stacey waved the waitress over to the table.

'No. My order.' Turning to the waitress she said, 'Strawberry Angel Delight and some humble pie for my pal here.'

'Sorry. You look nothing like a stripper,' Liam mumbled.

'How many you seen then?' Stacey teased.

'None, no, only in films like.'

'Films?' Stacey tried to keep her lips from smiling.

'Not films, like films. Films like old stuff, *Showgirls*, not really strippers at all.'

'Never mind.' Stacey's lips turned upwards. 'Is this a date?'

'Not sure, I mean, I asked you out so I suppose it is.'

'How long you here for?'

'Oh, start at six.'

'I mean, in Glasgow, how long you in Glasgow for?'

'Maybe a couple of weeks, depends how I get on.'

'Get on with what?'

Liam made a Demerara mountain in the sugar bowl

Stacey reached for his hand and took the teaspoon. 'We've all got secrets.'

'Not like this. It's family stuff and all a bit too weird. I'm having trouble getting to grips with it myself, let alone share it with anyone.'

'Fair enough, but I'm here when you're ready.'

Chapter 42

Wredd walked the length of Sauchiehall Street twice before he found the small alleyway. It was dark and musty with overflowing wheelie bins and empty bottles strewn across the cobbles.

The door entry on the front close was boarded up with a diversion sign around to the back. There were various names taped on and beside the entry buttons. O'Hanlon wasn't one of them. Wredd looked again at the information from Carol.

First floor left. Wredd climbed the stairs and knocked on the half-open storm door. He heard music coming from the flat. He waited and this time banged the frosted glass of the inner door. A young man with dark skin and afro curls stumbled from the dark hallway to unlock the front door. Wredd started his prepared speech but was cut off as the young man turned and wandered back down the hall leaving Wredd standing on the doorstep.

'In you come, man.' The young man's voice sounded Jamaican. 'Ain't no prison, all this locking things up. Crazy.'

'Thanks!' Wredd called.

There were six doors in the hallway. Each with a number, all but one with a name-plate. Wredd dismissed the door the young man disappeared through and checked the others;

Lin Yung, Stefan Zpeweski, Lisa Jackson, Mohamed Asiefh.

Flat 1C looked promising. Wredd was about to knock when he heard a key turn from inside. He stepped back into the shadows.

The silhouette of a young man morphed in the doorway, a strip of light from the room he'd left making his physique look broader than it was. Wredd couldn't make out his features.

Liam carried a bin bag of rubbish. He wedged an umbrella in the doorway and headed off down the main stairs.

Wredd looked around quickly almost wetting himself with excitement. Should he look inside? What was he looking for?

How long before the boy came back?

Before Wredd finished considering his options Liam came whistling back up the close. Wredd pressed his back against the far wall and held his breath.

As the door of 1C closed, Wredd's lungs opened and he breathlessly tiptoed past the storm doors. At least he now knew where the boy was. He could hardly wait to break the news to Bernice.

* * *

Once he was back at Nick's, Wredd pulled a sheet of paper from beside his makeshift bed. His left hand was clammy as he held the pen and began to write. He was conscious of the gold band on his finger and shrugged off any feelings of betrayal to Maggie.

Nick walked in. Wredd pulled a magazine over the notepad.

'Love letters?' Nick looked around the room shifting piles of newspapers and clothes. 'Good for you. A few roses might do the trick. Women love flowers, chocs, that sort of thing.'

'It's a grocery list,' Wredd replied. 'Anyway, Maggie is in the wrong here, she won't be getting anything from me till she comes to her senses.'

'If you say so. Aha!' Nicked lifted a bunch of keys. 'Need to hang these around my waist like a jailer. You don't need groceries. You eat here.'

Nick went back into the bar. A moment later Wredd answered a knock on his door.

McIntosh stood in the doorway. 'Not going to invite me in?'

He remained standing as Wredd shifted some of his clothes from the sofa.

'Missing a woman's touch eh?' McIntosh straightened his tie. 'Leave them to it. Those two are bad news, Wredd. From what I hear, you have more spunk. I've some courier work I could put your way. Good money and all the women you could wish for.

Love the poms over there.'

'Australia?' Nick asked.

'Eventually.' McIntosh paused. 'A few stop offs here and there.' He lit a cigar. 'Real good money for the right man. You can retire in the sun. Wherever you choose.'

'What are the risks?' Wredd asked.

'What's to lose?' McIntosh replied.

Wredd tipped his cigarette against the written note and watched the flames consume his words.

'Tell me more.'

Chapter 43

Bernice stood at her kitchen window settling a milk carton on the worktop. She breathed heavily on the cold glass. Drawing her finger through the mist she wrote "Granny", and watched the letters dissolve with the condensation. The room felt icy cold. She knew then. She knew.

One call to the local post office and Mrs McEwan was delighted to share the sad tidings. Bernice could hear the excitement in the old woman's voice when she realised it was the wayward offspring of the deceased on the other end of the line.

'Oh, she would have been so pleased to hear from you. Of course it's too late now.'

Bernice swallowed. 'I need the details.'

'Never the same, bad enough losing your mother, then you leaving so sudden like. I suppose you made a better life for yourself. Broke the old dearie's heart.'

'Take it the service will be at St Margaret's? What time?'

'Hard life, poor wummin, poor sowell. Oh, two o'clock on Thursday. So you'll be bringing your man? How many little uns you have now?'

Noting the time and place of Granny's funeral on the back of her hand Bernice hung up the phone with Mrs McEwan still chattering on the line.

Bernice gripped the biro. She dug it deeply into her arm, scoring the flesh. The black ink stained her skin as Bernice folded to her knees.

* * *

Maggie once more fought a blinding headache. Gulping a glass of water, she pushed two paracetamol to the back of her throat.

'What's up?' Stacey was attracted to the kitchen by the

banging of doors, and pulling out of drawers.

'Tired, just tired.'

Stacey pressed the telephone answer machine.

"Bernice here, troops! I'm nipping away for a few days, not sure where I am staying but I will be back soon. Take care of Hex till I get home would you? Thanks!"

'Off where?' Stacey asked.

'Off her head if you ask me.'

'I am asking you.'

'Look, I need to nip out for a bit.'

'Mum?' Stacey looked directly at her. 'Want me to come with you?'

'It's nothing. It's fine. Bernice isn't going anywhere.'

* * *

Maggie caught up with Bernice at the train station. 'You can't rush over there on a whim.'

'Granny's gone. She's gone, Maggie.' Bernice dabbed a tissue at her eyes.

'What! How did you find out?'

'Intuition. I'm going, Maggie. I need to go.'

'I'm coming with you. I'll call Stacey from the ferry terminal; grab a toothbrush at the next station. Need to let Wredd know too.'

'Don't worry about Wredd, or McIntosh either. They are out of your life; I've made sure that they are.'

Further along the carriage, Dermott sat beside a tearful Liam. The young man struggled to hold back his tears.

'Look, son,' Dermott spoke softly. 'I know it's hard, but she didn't suffer, just slipped away.'

'Didn't suffer?'

A few passengers raised their eyes.

'Didn't suffer? Maybe not in death, but we both know how

much she suffered in life.'

'You need to calm down. The old man doesn't know you left the island.'

'I'll tell him. I'll tell him why too.'

'Liam, there's no point. Bernadette probably moved on a long time ago. You two are strangers to each other.'

'We are family Dermott. Bernadette is family.'

Bernice wept quietly as Maggie held her hand. Both women sat in silence throughout the journey.

The man stayed on the upper deck. He kept watch over all four of them. This wasn't in the plan. He wanted to approach Bernice alone, not have to fight for her attention. She must be curious about the baby, young as she was at the time, she must wonder. Typical of that stupid old woman to bow out before the deal was closed. Auld O'Hanlon was right. Bad stock the lot of them.

Chapter 44

The ferry berthed with an hour to spare. Most passengers rushed off to be collected by friends and family. Bernice held back. Maggie nudged her friend.

'We need to find out how to get there, to the farm.'

'Not going to the farm.'

'What? Where are we going?'

'Told you. Granny has passed over. We're going to the funeral.'

'But you said your intuition told you?'

'Yes, and the local fishwife confirmed it last night.'

'Oh, Bernice. I know how much you wanted to sort things out with her.'

'I will. Not in this life, but I will. We'll cadge a lift from the skipper's mate.'

Chapter 45

The church looked small and derelict from a distance, but up close it oozed tired warmth. Maggie briefly hugged Bernice and made her way towards the open doors leaving her friend standing in the shadow of the trees.

Beetles of sweat trickled like broken rosary beads to the base of Bernice's spine. A carpet of leaves spread before her. Autumn was coming to a close. The bronze and terracotta mosaic of nature turning dark and unrecognisable.

The crunch of tyres on gravel distracted her thoughts. Flanked by two men, Granddad was helped from the car. Bernice recognised Robbie and Dermott, her childhood enemies. Tall and broad with hair as black as the ravens circling the sky above, carbon copies of the man Granddad used to be. She failed to notice a younger man struggling for composure in the back seat of the hired car. Robbie and Dermott brought Granddad steadily to his feet with a firm grip.

'Scorpions guarding a special treasure,' Bernice mumbled. 'Smaller than I remember.'

His hair tumbled in white whispers across his brow, grey skin as withered as the leaves beneath her feet.

His entourage was gathered for the event, huddled under dark umbrellas, like slithering snails cowering under clusters of mushrooms. Tossing her cigarette to the ground, Bernice crushed it underfoot. He cast a brief glance in her direction. She saw no flicker of recognition. The significance of the moment was lost. Many hands reached out to him offering comfort and condolences. A dark coat was draped around his shoulders; cloak for a king. Guided towards the church, his cronies followed until they disappeared like rats down a sewer.

The hearse snaked into the short driveway shrouded by a mantilla of rain. It crawled slowly towards its destination. As the darkened sky wept, a sharp wind hacked at Bernice's ankles. Trees bowed in respect. It was the ideal vantage point and she was reluctant to move from it.

A swarm of bodies seeped into the church. Bernice merged discreetly with the shadowy figures, her head lowered. Standing behind the main throng of the congregation she slowly began the task of identifying the mourners. Curiosity satisfied, Bernice slid onto the end of the back pew where Maggie sat.

'Bluebells?' Maggie asked.

Bernice clutched the freshly plucked flowers protectively on her lap, ignoring the dark soil weeping from their roots.

A flush-faced priest began his well-worn sermon; hands trembling as he eagerly awaited his next taste of communion wine.

Bernice's mind was elsewhere.

The choir sang out of tune as Maggie slipped her hand under Bernice's elbow. 'Bernice?'

The crowd knelt on the worn pews.

'Devoted wife and mother...sadly missed by all who knew her...'

Maggie put her arm around Bernice's shoulder. 'You okay?'

Bernice dabbed at her eyes. 'Not a word about me,' she whispered.

The sermon was coming to a close. Bernice shivered as her coat clung to her, cold and damp, a clammy hand pushing her to make her next move.

The cavalcade of hypocrites shuffled to their feet. Bernice waited until Granddad rose then wedged herself in the doorway, blocking his exit. He faltered for a moment and with an air of impatience, raised his walking stick.

'Out of my way, bloody eejit.' Catching the stick mid blow, Bernice stared into his face and realised that she never knew his eyes were brown. He snorted with confused anger.

'Who the hell do you think you are!' Gnarled hands like

anaemic spiders groped around for the stick. The muttering surrounding them subsided to hushed whispers as the circle of predators tightened around her.

Gripped by a fit of familiar coughing, the old man clutched at his chest as he tried to regain his stature. Reaching down for the fallen stick, Bernice smiled. Tightening her grip on the handle of the cane, she leaned closer.

She recognised the scent of stale whisky on his breath as she whispered, 'You broke Granny's heart. But you never broke her spirit, and that was her legacy to me.'

As the old man stammered her name, Robbie lurched forwards, loosening Granddad's collar, frantically looking around for help.

'Someone call an ambulance!'

The mourners gathered around Robbie and the old man. Dermott approached Bernice. 'I never knew. Honestly, I never knew.' He rested his hand on her arm and squeezed. 'Come back to the house? Please.'

Chapter 46

The main throng of mourners mingled awkwardly in the lounge bar of the Pig and Bull, picking at spongy sausage rolls; silence broken by whispered conversations peppered with forced subtle laughter, people shifting from foot to foot, taking an unnatural interest in the faded wallpaper. Maggie nodded, shook hands and gulped at her Merlot, leaving a strange purple shadow around her trembling lips. She craned her neck looking for Bernice.

'Gone off and left you has she?' Mrs McEwan sidled up beside Maggie and extended her hand. 'Mrs McEwan, postmistress and proprietor. Popped over to pay my respects.'

Maggie accepted the handshake, taken aback when Mrs McEwan tightened her grip. The older lady leaned close to Maggie and blew secrets into her hair.

After she walked away, Maggie staggered slightly and grabbed the bar for support.

'You alright, missy?' The face looked familiar despite the scarf looped around half of the man's face. Maggie felt hot and thought she might pass out.

Next thing she was aware of was a tumbler of cold water being pressed into her hand.

'Better, missy?' His face. His voice. Maggie still felt faint.

'Thank you, yes, I'm wondering about the last ferry? I, we, need to be getting back.'

'Nonsense, been a while since Bernadette visited, I'm sure someone can put you up for the night.'

Maggie shivered at the idea.

'The old fella didn't make it.' Mrs McEwan rushed breathlessly back into the room. 'Robbie called from the infirmary. Lad's in bits.'

Maggie felt a hand on her shoulder and turned to see Nick with Stacey not far behind.

'What are you two doing here? Is Wredd with you?'

They both shook their head.

'I'll away up the farm and let them know,' a voice bellowed.

'What's the story here then?' Nick asked. 'Stacey begged me to bring her over, something happen with Bernice?'

'Her granny, isn't it obvious?'

'Knew it was some sort of wake. Poor Bernice, where is she?'

'Away up to the farm apparently, with one of those brothers of hers.'

'She hasn't got any brothers.'

'Step-brothers then. What does it matter, Nick? This place gives me the creeps. We need to find Bernice and get out of here.'

The room fell silent as Bernice walked through the main door straight to the bar. She went behind the bar and pulled at the cord of a big brass bell.

'Good to be back! Missed me have you! Anyone anything they want to say? Oh, maybe if I turn my back. Make it easier for you, eh? Don't fret. I'm not one to bear a grudge, not with you lot, only him, my dear old granddad.'

Dermott went to Bernice and moved her gently to the front of the bar. Nick stepped in and ushered her over to Stacey and Maggie.

'It's over then. Granny's gone and. He'll never get near her now.'

'I want you to meet someone, Bernice, come through to the back,' Dermott asked quietly.

Maggie and Stacey each took an arm as Nick followed. Dermott showed them into a parlour. A huge wingback leather chair sat near a tall fireplace. Liam rose and turned to face the small group.

'Liam?' Stacey stepped towards him, Nick held her back.

Bernice stared hard at Liam. 'What are you doing here?'

'It's your barman, Nick.' Maggie leaned against the wall.

'You're seeing Stacey aren't you?' Nick asked.

'Yes,' Liam said quietly, 'but there is a stronger connection here.' He walked towards Bernice and held out his hands. Robbie came quietly into the room and stood behind Dermott.

Bernice looked closely at Liam: his pale freckled skin, copper hair.

'No way!' Bernice cried.

The door crashed open and Tam McShane tumbled in. He was drunk. Dermott and Robbie moved to push him back into the lounge.

'McShane!' Bernice croaked.

'I knew I'd seen you before,' Maggie spoke hurriedly. 'Oh, Bernice I didn't want to tell you, but he came to the flat. He wrote the letters.'

'I doubt that,' Dermott said. 'This aul drunk can't read or write.'

'Then who?' Maggie asked.

'Wredd did a lot of scribbling before he got tied into crime with that McIntosh.'

'Dad?' Stacey sniffled. 'Is it not bad enough he's moved abroad? You want to blacken his reputation?'

Bernice turned to Maggie.

'You never told him?' Bernice was too tired to argue. 'Makes sense though, with his debts, but he must have known I don't have cash to spare?'

'Wredd wouldn't know anything about the burial.' Maggie moved closer to Nick. 'There are a few things Wredd never knew about.'

'So? Liar, blackmailer, thief.'

'Mum? What burial? You mean today, Bernice's granny?'

'No, Stacey. I'll explain later, now isn't the time.'

'Maybe you can let me into the secret too?' Nick shook his head. 'Letters, burials, him away auditioning as a drug mule.'

'What!' Stacey cried. Nick hugged her and looked over her shoulder at Maggie. 'Some father you picked out for your daughter.'

'He's not...' Maggie sighed.

Bernice looked at Maggie and then at Nick. Maggie nodded and put her finger to her lips.

McShane spoke proudly. 'I don't know anything about any letters. I bought a headstone. Best there is.'

'What's going on here?' Bernice looked from one to another. 'Headstone for whom?'

'Your son, Bernadette. I lost these two.' He pointed at Dermott and Robbie. 'I'm dying, I'm begging your forgiveness.' He dropped to his knees.

'You can beg till your knees bleed. I'll never forgive you for ruining my life and Granny's.'

Liam stepped closer to Bernice and took her hands in his. 'I came looking for you. Seems I wasn't the only one.'

'I don't understand.' Bernice touched Liam's cheek.

Stacey sobbed loudly as Nick tried to comfort her. McShane roared. 'We buried him, same night, glad to be rid truth be known, but now, my days are numbered. I need your forgiveness.' He turned to the group one by one. 'All of you. Please. I'm an old man. A stupid old man. I have nothing.'

Nick hushed the group. 'What the fuck is going on here?'

'You are McShane? You came back after all this time and conned money of her?' Maggie pushed the old man and he stumbled. 'Now you're lying about a tombstone? Where is it then? What have you buried? A pigeon? A dead dog?'

Dermott was the first to speak. 'You are past forgiveness. Nothing, and I mean NOTHING can ever make up for what you did. I hope you rot in hell, Father, but not before suffering a long and painful death.'

Mrs MacEwan slipped into the room and sat listening closely. She smiled at Maggie. Robbie tugged Dermott's sleeve.

'Oh, I think you'll find neither McShane nor your fella Wredd wrote any letters.'

They all turned to look the old woman. Mrs MacEwan revelled in the attention.

'Truth will come out,' she said. 'You been through your granny's effects, Bernadette?'

'All in good time. What are you getting at?'

'You'll find out when the time is right.'

'Can't we take him in?' Robbie ignored Mrs MacEwan's cryptic statement.

'No, Robbie. Because of that excuse for humanity we have all been living a lie. We didn't bury our ma today. She died a long time ago, driven to an early grave by that bastard. It is Liam who should be chief mourner today.'

'Bernice you mean?' Nick asked.

'You're not him.' Bernice looked closely at Liam. 'I thought for a minute?'

'I'm your brother, Bernadette.' Liam cried freely.

'She doesn't have a brother,' Nick said.

'Born two months after you left for Glasgow.' Dermott laid a hand on her sleeve.

'Wow!' Bernice stumbled and fell onto a chair. 'Brother? Stop messing with my head.'

'Liam?' Stacey wiped the tears from her face.

'This is all too weird,' Nick said.

'Granny was in her late forties, Nick.' Bernice laughed. 'I don't know why my Humiel was taken, but I am thankful that Liam survived. When I think back, Granny did seem to be piling on the weight. I just thought she was keeping me company, eating for two. That old pinnie of hers hid a lot. '

'Humiel?' Stacey asked.

'My son, I called him Humiel, it means "angel of dignity".' Bernice spoke to McShane. 'But with your bad blood poisoning his system it's no wonder the lad couldn't face a world with you in it. Passed over. Only way he could be free of you.'

'Help me get him out of here,' Dermott told Robbie. The two

brothers dragged the protesting McShane from the room.

'We'll stay. Celebrate.'

'Bernice, I don't think that's a good idea?' Maggie said.

'Rubbish. We'll stay. I'll visit Humiel's grave. Then we'll have a party. A great big party to celebrate my family being back together. Me with a brother? You have taste, Stacey. Just pray he is nothing like his old man.'

'None of us are,' Dermott said. 'We will make up for lost time, Bernadette. Gran will be laid to rest with your mother. I'll see to it that Humiel is too. The plot is covered in bluebells in a shaded corner. I'll take you there, whenever you want, Bernadette.'

'Bernice. Please. Bernadette is long gone.'

Chapter 48

Whilst Maggie was downstairs dealing with the catering, Bernice was getting ready to join the party. All of the villagers were invited along with friends from Glasgow.

Bernice ran her tongue along the sticky flap of the velum envelope. The razor edge sliced deliciously through the soft flesh of her upper lip. Ruby droplets stained the creamy surface as she flinched slightly for a moment, before shivering with delight. Her words would be protected by the soft waxy seal she placed firmly on the back. Bernice hesitated, *Who did write the letters about Humiel?* This was still a mystery to her.

She slid her letter between selections of books. This occasion required a formal note of thanks.

Her gown hung on the back of the bedroom door. Shaking a curtain of glossed ringlets, she stooped forwards and let the garment spill over porcelain skin; her body, although slim, no longer taut with youth; ample breasts with nipples stiffening, as the materials sensuously brushed against her skin; layers of soft black lace, whispers of thin velvet ribbon woven through the delicate fabric.

A cobweb of fine silk threads plunged from the neckline to the base of her spine, falling in a soft curve above the henna tattoo that kissed her skin.

Her veil of curls shimmered in the moonlight, as she stood by the bay window and pulled back the voile, just enough to confirm the night's descent. She felt the soft breeze caress her.

Their guests began to arrive. Bernice watched in silence as cars snuffed headlights before resting in haphazard rows, like corpses on a battlefield. Bernice heard music drift up the stairs.

A few guests turned as she glided down the stairway with deliberate steady steps, pausing only to smile and scan the room of familiar faces.

Bernice made her entrance calmly and folded into the crowd, graciously exchanging pleasantries and hugs, gradually snaking a path towards the kitchen.

Maggie was busily arranging the platters with food from the oven.

'You look a million dollars.' She welcomed Bernice's late arrival. Resting a tray of vol-au-vents on a butcher's block, she leaned over and hugged Bernice tightly.

'Honestly, you are sparkling.' She glanced at Bernice from head to toe, genuinely pleased her earlier signs of apprehension about the party appeared to have vanished.

'I'll be fine on my own. Honest, I'll manage.' Maggie ushered Bernice back towards the living room. Her words poignant to Bernice's ears.

'Whits yir poison the night?' Stacey tottered across the room, wielding a half-empty bottle of Moet. 'Champagne Charlie?'

She thrust a fizzing flute into Bernice's hand, looping her bottle-carrying arm around the older woman's neck; Stacey raised her voice above the chatter. 'Let's get this party staaaarted.'

A slobbery kiss landed affectionately on Bernice's cheek. Stacey gyrated her way into the centre of the room, followed by Liam. Bernice never touched the drink. The evening flowed easily, guests gradually losing interest in Bernice, they broke into huddles, dancing and chatting. Nick was in a huddle with Dermott and Robbie. Bernice lay the champagne glass down, and lifted her pashmina from the sideboard before heading discreetly out of the front door.

She fastened the wrap with a silver brooch and strolled to the end of the road where Maggie parked her hire car earlier to leave space for the revellers.

'Seen Bernice?' Maggie asked her bobbing daughter.

'Nope. Maybe gone upstairs for a wee lie doon. Getting on you know.'

'Should I go up and check on her?' Maggie asked Nick.

'No. Let her rest. She'll come back down in her own time.' Nick brushed his finger against Maggie's cheek. 'You enjoy the party. It's your celebration too now Wredd's gone. Idiot excuse of a man.'

Bernice drove away from the farm and didn't look back. Focused on reaching her destination, she followed the familiar route until it joined with the narrow coastal road.

The short journey gave her time to reflect on her life, and the decision she was about to take.

Standing on the beach she let the sand trickle over her bare feet. She rocked gently, softly breathing a lullaby, and looked out at the idyllic sea-scape. The bewitching hour was close.

Bernice ambled along the shoreline. A lone figure, she settled at the mouth of a cave. Scraping the cushion of a thumb through damp sand, a circle of protection was cast. Slivers of moonlight drizzled over pebbles and shells offered by the glittering waters. Anxiously fingering the silver clasp at her neck she loosened the clasp, and stepped out of her gown, revealing her nakedness to the harvest moon. A wreath of lotus buds tangled with fiery curls, crowning her shadowy silhouette. As the velvet of the night caressed her trembling body she channelled her energies, and the fertility ritual began.

She cupped the candles in quivering hands and gave life to the flames. With arms outstretched she welcomed the fall of the moon on her upturned face. Her whispered wishes implored the deities to grant Stacey a long and loving life with Liam and a safe journey towards motherhood. Bernice's gift to them.

Oblivious to the pierce of lightning lost on the horizon, Bernice snuffed out the glow of the candle with a sigh, and silently erased her presence from the scene. She looked towards the open space and saw her mother, beside her Granny stood holding Humiel in the crochet shawl.

A cloak of darkness wrapped comfortingly around her. In the

distance a cat purred. Bernice remembered Stacey's words, and decided not to swim against the tide any longer. She waded into the cool water and let the waves take her to her destiny.

The beginning...

Bernice's poem to Humiel

My Son

They gave me drugs to make me sleep
And said, "You're only young."
For days I would lie down and weep,
For the songs you never sang.

Proud mothers pass me, pushing prams
My eyes and throat are raw.
Toddlers asleep in their mother's arms
And the flowers you never saw.

I touch the grass and breathe fresh air.
I feel my soul will melt.
I can't explain the utter despair
Or the rain you never felt.

I can't describe a rainbow
And I just can't quite believe,
You'll never get the chance to feel,
The magic of Hallow's Eve.

So, although we never met
And I never spoke your name,
I swear I won't forget,
And love you just the same.

At Roundfire we publish great stories. We lean towards the spiritual and thought-provoking. But whether it's literary or popular, a gentle tale or a pulsating thriller, the connecting theme in all Roundfire fiction titles is that once you pick them up you won't want to put them down.